PUFFIN BOOKS

More Stories for Seven-Year-Olds

Sara and Stephen Corrin's anthologies of stories have proved enormously popular in Puffin with both children and parents. Perhaps most popular of all is *Stories for Seven-Year-Olds*, which was their first collection. It's marvellous then that the Corrins have now edited a second book for children of seven or thereabouts, that magical age when they are ready to be introduced to the whole range of folk and fairy tale.

There are traditional tales from Ireland, Greece, Russia, Italy and Canada, in which the dreadful deeds of kings, witches, monsters and dragons are expounded. There are also modern stories from authors like Rudyard Kipling, Joan Aiken and James Reeves. Add the names of Hans Andersen and Arthur Ransome, and you have the perfect recipe for a spellbinding collection of stories!

Sara Corrin has made the subject of children's responses to literature one of her main studies. She is a Senior Lecturer in Education and specializes in child development. Born within the sound of Bow Bells, she has all the Cockney's good humour and jaunty repartee. Stephen, her husband, was brought up on a mixed diet of the *Gem*, the *Magnet*, the Bible, cricket and Beethoven quartets. He reviews, writes stories and translates from French, Russian, German and Danish.

More Stories for Seven-Year-Olds

and other young readers

EDITED BY
SARA AND STEPHEN CORRIN

Illustrated by Shirley Hughes

Puffin Books
in association with Faber and Faber Ltd

PUFFIN BOOKS

Published by the Penguin Group
27 Wrights Lane, London w8 5TZ, England
Viking Penguin Inc., 40 West 23rd Street, New York, New York 10010, USA
Penguin Books Australia Ltd, Ringwood, Victoria, Australia
Penguin Books Canada Ltd, 2801 John Street, Markham, Ontario, Canada L3R 1B4
Penguin Books (NZ) Ltd, 182–190 Wairau Road, Auckland 10, New Zealand

Penguin Books Ltd, Registered Offices: Harmondsworth, Middlesex, England

First published by Faber and Faber Ltd 1978
Published in Puffin Books 1982
13 15 17 19 20 18 16 14 12

Printed in England by Clays Ltd, St Ives plc
Filmset in Monophoto Baskerville

Contents

Contents

A Word to the Story-Teller

Seven is a magic number.

The spells of fairy tales last for seven years. 'For seven years and a day we have wandered over the world.' 'For seven long years and a day shall you serve me.'

It is no old wives' tale that we renew ourselves, so to speak, in seven-yearly cycles, and it is around the age of seven that children are ready for the great adventures into the unknown. Their minds are eager to roam the vast world of the imagination. Fantasy is there for the asking and the more they are given, the greater their enjoyment. They, too, will fall under the spell when they read these tales.

Our earlier *Stories for Seven-Year-Olds and other Young Readers* was so favourably received that we have responded to the demand for more, and our new collection draws on the folklore of many countries.

The Fiery Dragon

The little white Princess always woke up in her little white bed when the starlings began to chatter in the pearl-grey morning. As soon as the woods were awake she used to run up the twisting turret-stairs with her little bare feet, and stand on the top of the tower in her white bed-gown, and kiss her hands to the sun and to the woods and to the sleeping town, and say: 'Good morning, pretty world!'

Then she would run down the cold stone steps and dress herself in her short skirt and her cap and apron, and begin the day's work. She swept the rooms and made the breakfast, she washed the dishes and she scoured the pans, and all this she did because she was a real Princess. For of all who should have served her, only one remained faithful – her old nurse, who had lived with her in the tower all the Princess's life. And, now the nurse was old and feeble, the Princess would not let her work any more but did all the housework herself while nurse sat still and did the sewing, because this was a real Princess with a skin like milk and hair like flax and a heart like gold.

Her name was Sabrinetta, and her grandmother was Sabra, who married St George after he had killed the dragon, and by real rights all the country belonged to her, the woods that stretched away to the mountains, and the downs that sloped down to the sea and the pretty fields of corn and maize and rye, the olive orchards and the vineyards, and the little town itself with its towers and its turrets, its steep roofs and strange windows, that nestled in the hollow between the sea where

9

the whirlpool was and the mountains, white with snow and rosy with sunrise.

But when her father and mother died, leaving her cousin to take care of the kingdom till she grew up, he, being a very evil Prince, had taken everything away from her, and all the people had followed him, and now nothing was left her of all her possessions except the great dragon-proof tower that her grandfather, St George, had built, and of all who should have been her servants, only the good nurse.

And this was why Sabrinetta was the first person in all the land to get a glimpse of the wonder.

Early, early, early, while all the townspeople were fast asleep, she ran up the turret-steps and looked out over the field, and at the other side of the field there is a green-ferny ditch and a rose-thorny hedge, and then comes the wood. And as Sabrinetta stood on her tower she saw a shaking and a twisting of the rose-thorny hedge, and then something very bright and shining wriggled out through it into the ferny ditch and back again. It only came out for a minute, but she saw it quite plainly, and she said to herself: 'Dear me, what a curious, shiny, bright-looking creature! If it were bigger, and if I didn't know that there have been no fabulous monsters for quite a long time now, I should almost think it was a dragon.'

The thing, whatever it was, did look rather like a dragon – but then it was too small; and it looked rather like a lizard – only then it was too big. It was about as long as a hearthrug.

'I wish it had not been in such a hurry to get back into the wood,' said Sabrinetta. 'Of course, it's quite safe for me, in my dragon-proof tower, but if it is a dragon, it's quite big enough to eat people, and today's the first of May, and the children go out to get flowers in the wood.'

When Sabrinetta had done the housework (she did not

leave so much as a speck of dust anywhere, even in the corneriest corner of the winding stair) she put on her milk-white silky gown with the moon-daisies worked on it, and went up to the top of her tower again.

Across the fields troops of children were going out to gather the may, and the sound of their laughter and singing came up to the top of the tower.

'I do hope it *wasn't* a dragon,' said Sabrinetta.

The children went by twos and by threes and by tens and by twenties, and the red and blue and yellow and white of their frocks were scattered on the green of the field.

'It's like a green silk mantle worked with flowers,' said the Princess, smiling.

By twos and by threes, by tens and by twenties, the children vanished into the wood, till the mantle of the field was left plain green once more.

'All the embroidery is unpicked,' said the Princess, sighing.

The sun shone, and the sky was blue, and the fields were quite green, and all the flowers were very bright indeed, because it was May Day.

Then quite suddenly a cloud passed over the sun, and the silence was broken by shrieks from afar off, and, like a many-coloured torrent, all the children burst from the wood, and rushed, a red and blue and yellow and white wave, across the field, screaming as they ran. Their voices came up to the Princess on her tower, and she heard the words threaded on their screams, like beads on sharp needles.

'The dragon, the dragon, the dragon! Open the gates! The dragon is coming! The fiery dragon!'

And they swept across the field and into the gate of the town, and the Princess heard the gate bang, and the children were out of sight – but on the other side of the field the rose-thorns crackled and smashed in the hedge, and something very large and glaring and horrible trampled the ferns in the ditch for one moment before it hid itself again in the covert of the wood.

The Princess went down and told her nurse, and the nurse at once locked the great door of the tower and put the key in her pocket.

'Let them take care of themselves,' she said, when the Princess begged to be allowed to go out and help to take care of the children.

'My business is to take care of you, my precious, and I'm going to do it. Old as I am, I can turn a key still.'

So Sabrinetta went up again to the top of her tower, and cried whenever she thought of the children and the fiery dragon. For she knew, of course, that the gates of the town were not dragon-proof, and that the dragon could just walk in whenever he liked.

The children ran straight to the palace, where the Prince was cracking his hunting-whip down at the kennels, and told him what had happened.

'Good sport,' said the Prince, and he ordered out his pack of hippopotamuses at once. It was his custom to hunt big game with hippopotamuses, and people would not have minded that so much – but he would swagger about in the streets of the town with his pack yelping and gambolling at his heels, and, when he did that, the greengrocer, who had his stall in the market-place, always regretted it; and the crockery merchant, who spread his wares on the pavement, was ruined for life every time the Prince chose to show off his pack.

The Prince rode out of the town with his hippopotamuses trotting and frisking behind him, and people got inside their houses as quickly as they could when they heard the voices of his pack and the blowing of his horn. The pack squeezed through the town gates and off across country to hunt the dragon. Few of you who have not seen a pack of hippopotamuses in full cry will be able to imagine at all what the hunt was like. To begin with, hippopotamuses do not bay like hounds, they grunt like pigs, and their grunt is very big and fierce. Then, of course, no one expects hippopotamuses to jump. They just crash through the hedges and lumber through the standing corn, doing serious injury to the crops, and annoying the farmers very much. All the hippopotamuses had collars with their name and address on, but when the farmers called at the palace to complain of the injury to their standing crops, the Prince always said it served them right for leaving their crops standing about in people's way, and he never paid anything at all.

So now, when he and his pack went out, several people in the town whispered, 'I wish the dragon would eat *him*' – which was very wrong of them, no doubt, but then he was such a very nasty Prince.

They hunted by field, and they hunted by wold; they drew the woods blank, and the scent didn't lie on the downs at all. The dragon was shy, and would not show himself.

But just as the Prince was beginning to think there was no dragon at all, but only a cock and bull, his favourite old hippopotamus gave tongue. The Prince blew his horn and shouted: 'Tally-ho! Hark forward! Tantivy!' and the whole pack charged downhill towards the hollow by the wood. For there, plain to be seen, was the dragon, as big as a barge, glowing like a furnace, and spitting fire and showing his shining teeth.

'The hunt is up!' cried the Prince. And indeed it was. For

the dragon – instead of behaving as a quarry should, and running away – ran straight at the pack, and the Prince on his elephant had the mortification of seeing his prize pack swallowed up one by one in the twinkling of an eye, by the dragon they had come out to hunt. The dragon swallowed all the hippopotamuses just as a dog swallows bits of meat. It was a shocking sight. Of the whole of the pack that had come out sporting so merrily to the music of the horn, now not even a puppy-hippopotamus was left, and the dragon was looking anxiously round to see if he had forgotten anything.

The Prince slipped off his elephant on the other side, and ran into the thickest part of the wood. He hoped the dragon could not break through the bushes there, since they were very strong and close. He went crawling, on hands and knees in a most un-Prince-like way, and, at last, finding a hollow tree, he crept into it. The wood was very still – no crashing of branches and no smell of burning came to alarm the Prince. He drained the silver hunting-bottle slung from his shoulder, and stretched his legs in the hollow tree. He never shed a single tear for his poor tame hippopotamuses who had eaten from his hand, and followed him faithfully in all the pleasures of the chase for so many years. For he was a false Prince, with a skin like leather and hair like hearth-brushes and a heart like stone. He never shed a tear, but he just went to sleep. When he awoke it was dark. He crept out of the tree and rubbed his eyes. The wood was black about him, but there was a red glow in a dell close by, and it was a fire of stocks, and beside it sat a ragged youth with long, yellow hair, and all round lay sleeping forms which breathed heavily.

'Who are you?' said the Prince.

'I'm Elfinn, the pig-keeper,' said the ragged youth. 'And who are you?'

'I'm Tiresome, the Prince,' said the other.

'And what are you doing out of your palace at this time of night?' asked the pig-keeper severely.

'I've been hunting,' said the Prince.

The pig-keeper laughed. 'Oh, it was you I saw, then? A good hunt, wasn't it? My pigs and I were looking on.'

All the sleeping forms grunted and snored, and the Prince saw that they were pigs: he knew it by their manners.

'If you had known as much as I do,' Elfinn went on, 'you might have saved your pack.'

'What do you mean?' said Tiresome.

'Why, the dragon,' said Elfinn. 'You went out at the wrong time of day. The dragon should be hunted at *night*.'

'No, thank you,' said the Prince, with a shudder. 'A day-light hunt is quite good enough for me, you silly pig-keeper.'

'Oh, well,' said Elfinn, 'do as you like about it – the dragon will come and hunt *you* tomorrow, as likely as not. I don't care if he does, you silly Prince.'

'You're very rude,' said Tiresome.

'Oh no, only truthful,' said Elfinn.

'Well, tell me the truth then. What is it that if I had known as much as you do about, I shouldn't have lost my hippo-potamuses?'

'You don't speak very good English,' said Elfinn; 'but, come, what will you give me if I tell you?'

'If you tell me what?' said the tiresome Prince.

'What you want to know.'

'I don't want to know anything,' said Prince Tiresome.

'Then you're more of a silly even than I thought,' said Elfinn. 'Don't you want to know how to settle the dragon before he settles you?'

'It might be as well,' the Prince admitted.

'Well, I haven't much patience at any time,' said Elfinn, 'and now I can assure you that there's very little left. What will you give me if I tell you?'

'Half my kingdom,' said the Prince, 'and my cousin's hand in marriage.'

'Done,' said the pig-keeper; 'here goes! *The dragon grows small at nights!* He sleeps under the root of this tree. I use him to light my fire with.'

And sure enough, there under the trees was the dragon on a nest of scorched moss, and he was about as long as your finger.

'How can I kill him?' asked the Prince.

'I don't know that you *can* kill him,' said Elfinn, 'but you can take him away if you've brought anything to put him in. That bottle of yours would do.'

So between them they managed, with bits of stick and by singeing their fingers a little, to poke and shove the dragon till they made it creep into the silver hunting-bottle and then the Prince screwed on the top tight.

'Now we've got him,' said Elfinn, 'let's take him home and put Solomon's seal on the mouth of the bottle, and then he'll be safe enough. Come along – we'll divide up the kingdom tomorrow, and then I shall have some money to buy fine clothes to go courting in.'

But when the wicked Prince made promises he did not make them to keep.

'Go on with you! What do you mean?' he said. 'I found the dragon and I've imprisoned him. I never said a word about courtings or kingdoms. If you say I did, I shall cut your head off at once.' And he drew his sword.

'All right,' said Elfinn, shrugging his shoulders. 'I'm better off than you are, anyhow.'

'What do you mean?' spluttered the Prince.

'Why, you've only got a kingdom (and a dragon), but I've got clean hands (and five-and-seventy fine black pigs).'

So Elfinn sat down again by his fire, and the Prince went home and told his Parliament how clever and brave he had been, and though he woke them up on purpose to tell them, they were not angry, but said:

'You are indeed brave and clever.' They knew what happened to people with whom the Prince was not pleased.

Then the Prime Minister solemnly put Solomon's seal on the mouth of the bottle, and the bottle was put in the treasury, which was made of solid copper, with walls as thick as Waterloo Bridge.

The bottle was set down among the sacks of gold, and the junior secretary to the junior clerk of the last Lord of the Treasury was appointed to sit up all night with it, and see if anything happened. The junior secretary had never seen a dragon, and what was more, he did not believe the Prince had ever seen a dragon either. The Prince had never been a really truthful boy, and it would have been just like him to bring home a bottle with nothing in it, and then to pretend that there was a dragon inside. So the junior secretary did not at all mind being left. They gave him the key, and when everyone in the town had gone back to bed he let in some of the junior secretaries from other Government departments, and they had a jolly game of hide-and-seek among the sacks of gold, and played marbles with the diamonds and rubies and pearls in the big ivory chests.

They enjoyed themselves very much, but by-and-by the copper treasury began to get warmer and warmer, and suddenly the junior secretary cried out, 'Look at the bottle!'

The bottle sealed with Solomon's seal had swollen to three

times its proper size, and seemed to be nearly red hot, and the air got warmer and warmer and the bottle bigger and bigger, till all the junior secretaries agreed that the place was too hot to hold them, and out they went, tumbling over each other in their haste, and just as the last got out and locked the door the bottle burst, and out came the dragon, very fiery, and swelling more and more every minute, and he began to eat the sacks of gold, and crunch up the pearls and diamonds and rubies as you do 'hundreds and thousands'.

By breakfast-time he had devoured the whole of the Prince's treasures, and when the Prince came along the street at about eleven, he met the dragon coming out of the broken door of the treasury, with molten gold still dripping from his jaws. Then the Prince turned and ran for his life, and as he ran towards the dragon-proof tower the little white Princess saw him coming, and she ran down and unlocked the door and let him in, and slammed the dragon-proof door in the fiery face of the dragon, who sat down and whined outside, because he wanted the Prince very much indeed.

The Princess took Prince Tiresome into the best room, and laid the cloth, and gave him cream and eggs and white grapes, and honey and bread, with many other things, yellow and white and good to eat, and she served him just as kindly as she would have done if he had been anyone else instead of the bad Prince who had taken away her kingdom and kept it for himself – because she was a true Princess and had a heart of gold.

When he had eaten and drunk he begged the Princess to show him how to lock and unlock the door, and the nurse was asleep, so there was no one to tell the Princess not to, and she did.

'You turn the key like this,' she said, 'and the door keeps

shut. But turn it nine times round the wrong way, and the door flies open.'

And so it did. And the moment it opened the Prince pushed the white Princess out of her tower, just as he had pushed her out of her kingdom, and shut the door. For he wanted to have the tower all for himself. And there she was in the street, and on the other side of the way the dragon was sitting whining, but he did not try to eat her, because – though the old nurse did not know it – dragons cannot eat white Princesses with hearts of gold.

The Princess could not walk through the streets of the town in her milky-silky gown with the daisies on it, and with no hat and no gloves, so she turned the other way, and ran out across the meadows, towards the wood. She had never been out of her tower before, and the soft grass under her feet felt like grass of Paradise.

She ran right into the thickest part of the wood, because she did not know what her heart was made of, and she was afraid of the dragon, and there in a dell she came on Elfinn and his five-and-seventy fine pigs. He was playing his flute, and around him the pigs were dancing cheerfully on their hind legs.

'Oh dear,' said the Princess, 'do take care of me. I am so frightened.'

'I will,' said Elfinn, putting his arms round her. 'Now you are quite safe. What were you frightened of?'

'The dragon,' she said.

'So it's got out of the silver bottle,' said Elfinn. 'I hope it's eaten the Prince.'

'No,' said Sabrinetta, 'but why?'

So he told her of the mean trick that the Prince had played him.

'And he promised me half his kingdom and the hand of his cousin the Princess,' said Elfinn.

'Oh dear, what a shame!' said Sabrinetta, trying to get out of his arms. 'How dared he?'

'What's the matter?' he asked, holding her tighter. 'It *was* a shame, or at least I thought so. But *now* he may keep his kingdom, half and whole, if I may keep what I have.'

'What's that?' asked the Princess.

'Why, you – my pretty, my dear,' said Elfinn, 'and as for the Princess, his cousin, forgive me, dearest heart, but when I asked for her I hadn't seen the real Princess, the only Princess, *my* Princess.'

'Do you mean me?' said Sabrinetta.

'Who else?' he asked.

'Yes, but five minutes ago you hadn't seen me!'

'Five minutes ago I was a pig-keeper – now I've held you in my arms. I'm a Prince, though I should have to keep pigs to the end of my days.'

'But you haven't asked *me*?' said the Princess.

'*You* asked *me* to take care of you,' said Elfinn, 'and I will – all my life long.'

So that was settled, and they began to talk of really important things, such as the dragon and the Prince, and all the time Elfinn did not know that this was the Princess, but he knew that she had a heart of gold and he told her so, many times.

'The mistake,' said Elfinn, 'was in not having a dragon-proof bottle. I see that now.'

'Oh, is that all?' said the Princess. 'I can easily get one of those – because everything in my tower is dragon-proof. We ought to do something to settle the dragon and save the little children.'

So she started off to get the bottle, and she would not let Elfinn come with her.

'If what you say is true,' she said, 'if you are sure that I have a heart of gold, the dragon won't hurt me, and somebody *must* stay with the pigs.'

Elfinn was quite sure, so he let her go.

She found the door of her tower open. The dragon had waited patiently for the Prince, and the moment he opened the door and came out, though he was only out for an instant to post a letter to his Prime Minister, saying where he was, and asking them to send the fire brigade to deal with the fiery dragon, the dragon ate him. Then the dragon went back to the wood, because it was getting near his time to grow small for the night.

So Sabrinetta went in and kissed her nurse, and made her a cup of tea and explained what was going to happen, and that she had a heart of gold, so the dragon couldn't eat her, and the nurse saw that, of course, the Princess was quite safe, and kissed her and let her go.

She took the dragon-proof bottle, made of burnished brass, and ran back to the wood, and to the dell where Elfinn was sitting among his sleek black pigs, waiting for her.

'I thought you were never coming back,' he said; 'you have been away a year, at least.'

The Princess sat down beside him among the pigs, and they held each other's hands till it was dark, and then the dragon came crawling over the moss, scorching it as he came, and getting smaller as he crawled, and curled up under the root of the tree.

'Now then,' said Elfinn, 'you hold the bottle,' then he poked and prodded the dragon with bits of stick till it crawled into the dragon-proof bottle. But there was no stopper.

'Never mind,' said Elfinn, 'I'll put my finger in for a stopper.'

'No, let me,' said the Princess, but of course, Elfinn would not let her. He stuffed his finger into the top of the bottle, and the Princess cried out:

'The sea – the sea – run for the cliffs!' And off they went, with the five-and-seventy pigs trotting steadily after them in a long, black procession.

The bottle got hotter and hotter in Elfinn's hands, because the dragon inside was puffing fire and smoke with all his might. Hotter, and hotter, and hotter, but Elfinn held on till they came to the cliff-edge, and there was the dark-blue sea, and the whirlpool going round and round.

Elfinn lifted the bottle high above his head and hurled it out between the stars and the sea, and it fell in the middle of the whirlpool.

'We've saved the country,' said the Princess. 'You've saved the little children. Give me your hands.'

'I can't,' said Elfinn; 'I shall never be able to take your dear hands again. My hands are burnt off.'

And so they were: there were only black cinders where his hands ought to have been. The Princess kissed them, and cried over them, and tore pieces of the silky-milky gown to tie them up with, and the two went back to the tower and told the nurse all about everything. And the pigs sat outside and waited.

'He is the bravest man in the world,' said Sabrinetta. 'He has saved the country and the little children; but, oh, his hands – his poor, dear, darling hands!'

Here the door of the room opened, and the oldest of the five-and-seventy pigs came in. It went up to Elfinn and rubbed itself against him with little, loving grunts.

'See the dear creature,' said the nurse, wiping away tears; 'it knows, it knows!'

Sabrinetta stroked the pig, because Elfinn had no hands for stroking or for anything else.

'The only cure for a dragon-burn,' said the old nurse, 'is pig's fat, and well that faithful creature knows it –'

'I wouldn't for a kingdom,' cried Elfinn, stroking the pig as best he could with his elbow.

'Is there no other cure?' asked the Princess.

Here another pig put its black nose in at the door, and then another and another, till the room was full of pigs, a surging mass of rounded blackness, pushing and struggling to get at Elfinn, and grunting softly in the language of true affection.

'There is *one* other,' said the nurse; 'the dear affectionate beasts – they all want to die for you.'

'What *is* the other cure?' said Sabrinetta anxiously.

'If a man is burnt by a dragon,' said the nurse, 'and a certain number of people are willing to die for him, it is enough if each should kiss the burn, and wish it well in the depths of his loving heart.'

'The number! The number!' cried Sabrinetta.

'Seventy-seven,' said the nurse.

'We have only seventy-five pigs,' said the Princess, 'and with me that's seventy-six!'

'It must be seventy-seven – and I really *can't* die for him, so nothing can be done,' said the nurse, sadly. 'He must have cork hands.'

'I knew about the seventy-seven loving people,' said Elfinn. 'But I never thought my dear pigs loved me so much as all this, and my dear, too – And of course, that only makes it more impossible. There's *one* other charm that cures dragon

24

burns, though; but I'd rather be burnt black all over than marry anyone but you, my dear, my pretty.'

'Why, who must you marry to cure your dragon burns?' asked Sabrinetta.

'A Princess. That's how St George cured *his* burns.'

'There now! Think of that!' said the nurse. 'And I never heard tell of that cure, old as I am.'

But Sabrinetta threw her arms round Elfinn's neck, and held him as thought she would never let him go.

'Then it's all right, my dear, brave, precious Elfinn,' she cried, 'for I *am* a Princess, and you shall be my Prince. Come along, nurse – don't wait to put on your bonnet. We'll go and be married this very moment.'

So they went, and the pigs came after, moving in stately blackness, two by two. And the minute he was married to the Princess, Elfinn's hands got quite well. And the people, who were weary of Prince Tiresome and his hippopotamuses, hailed Sabrinetta and her husband as rightful Sovereigns of the land.

Next morning the Prince and Princess went out to see if the dragon had been washed ashore. They could see nothing of him; but when they looked out towards the whirlpool they saw a cloud of steam; and the fishermen reported that the water for miles around was hot enough to shave with! And as the water is hot there to this day, we may feel pretty sure that the fierceness of that dragon was such that all the waters of all the sea were not enough to cool him. The whirlpool is too strong for him to be able to get out of it, so there he spins round and round for ever and ever, doing some useful work at last, and warming the water for poor fisherfolk to shave with.

The Prince and Princess rule the land well and wisely. The nurse lives with them, and does nothing but fine sewing, and only that when she wants to very much. The Prince keeps no hippopotamuses, and is consequently very popular. The five-and-seventy devoted pigs live in white marble sties with brass knockers and 'Pig' on the door-plate, and are washed twice a day with Turkish sponges and soap scented with violets, and no one objects to their following the Prince when he walks abroad, for they behave beautifully, and always keep to the footpath, and obey the notices about not walking on the grass.

The Princess feeds them every day with her own hands, and her first edict on coming to the throne was that the word 'Pork' should never be uttered on pain of death, and should, besides, be scratched out of all the dictionaries.

The Giant's Stairs

On the Irish coast, near the cliff of Carrigmahon, you'll find the Giant's Stairs, made of huge rocks piled one on top of the other. Somewhere, hidden among the topmost rocks, high above the sea, so people said, the giant Mahon Macmahon lived in a cave.

It was just by the Giant's Stairs that Philip Ronayne disappeared quite suddenly, when he was only seven years of age.

His father and mother had nobody else in the world they loved more dearly. They searched the whole countryside, but no one had seen him. Had he fallen off a cliff, or had he been stolen away? No one claimed the handsome reward that they offered for his return. Months and years passed and still they searched, but no trace could be found. At last they gave up all hope of ever seeing their boy again.

Now close by the Ronayne home, not far from the cliff of Carrigmahon, lived Robin Kelly, a clever blacksmith, who not only made first-class ploughshares, but could also tell people the meaning of their dreams. Anybody who had a strange dream, and was worried by it, would come to Robin and he would explain just what it meant.

Exactly seven years to the day after Philip Ronayne had vanished, Robin himself had a most peculiar dream. In this dream the boy Philip appeared on a white horse and told the blacksmith how he had been spirited away to the giant Macmahon's cave high up in the rocks above the cliff of Carrigmahon and had been his page ever since. For seven whole years he had served the giant, but now, he said, his time of service could well be over if only Robin were bold and brave enough to try to set him free. Then Robin, still in his sleep, said, 'Tell me, Philip, how am I to know this is not simply a dream.' 'You shall know by this sign,' said the boy, and as he spoke the white horse gave Robin a kick on his forehead with one of his hooves, and the poor blacksmith awoke, shouting and screaming in fright and pain, thinking his head must be split open . . . and there on his forehead was the red mark made by the horse's hoof.

Now Robin, like everybody else in the district, knew the story of the giant Macmahon, and he had often been in his boat round the foot of the rocks where the giant was said to live. Many a time he had wondered whether Macmahon was somewhere up there, hidden from human eyes.

Robin told no one about his dream but he thought about it from morning till night, day in day out. At last he made up his mind that he must discover whether the dream meant anything. For if Philip had been spirited away by the giant, then Robin Kelly had clearly been summoned to bring him back.

So one evening, taking his ploughshare with him, he set out in his boat for the Giant's Stairs. His friend, Tom Clancy, went with him and they took turns to row as far as the foot of the cliff of Carrigmahon. Robin knew the cave could be seen only at midnight, if ever at all, for though everybody talked about the giant and his cave, no man had ever seen them. For a long time they looked for an entrance to a passage in the rocks, and towards midnight, just as Robin was beginning to think he must be chasing a dream, a faint light appeared, which grew brighter as time went on. They rowed to the spot where the light seemed to come from, and saw a porch wide enough for a horse to pass through. Robin stepped on to the rocky stairway which led up to the porch. In the eerie light the rocks took on the most terrifying shapes – gargoyle faces, misshapen heads, dragon-like teeth. Frightened as he was, he made his way along the passage that led to the cave, and found himself in front of a doorway leading to an immense room.

Inside he could see a table of solid rock and sitting around it a band of giants, so motionless that they too appeared to be made of rock. At the head of the table sat the largest giant, a long white beard covering his massive chest. Suddenly he looked up and glared at Robin.

'This must be Mahon Macmahon himself,' thought Robin, trembling with fear.

'What brings you here to this cave where no other man has dared to venture?' thundered the giant.

'I have come for Philip Ronayne. For seven long years he has served you and now the time is up,' said Robin bravely, though his knees were knocking, his teeth chattering and his hands trembling.

'Very well,' said the giant. 'You may have him if you can pick him out from among all the pages who serve me. But if you fail to pick him out you will lose your life.'

'There's no turning back now,' thought Robin. Mahon Macmahon led him into a huge hall, brilliantly lit, and there Robin saw hundreds of pages, all looking exactly alike – all the same age and all dressed in the same way. Poor Robin was at a loss; how was he to tell which one was Philip Ronayne? He had never known young Philip well, nor had he seen him for seven long years. He decided to play for time. 'How fine your page boys look!' he said to the giant. 'They must be well cared for.' The giant smiled grimly and stretched out his hand to thank Robin for the compliment. But Robin, instead of offering his own hand, held out his ploughshare. The giant twisted the iron with his fingers as though it were no tougher than a hairpin, and all the pageboys roared with laughter. All? No, not all. Robin, watching attentively, noticed that one boy was staring gloomily ahead, not a muscle in his face moving. Robin sprang forward and placed his hand firmly on the boy's shoulder.

'This is Philip Ronayne,' he cried, 'and if I lie let me die for it.'

There was a deafening crash and all the lights went out. Robin found himself on the cliff edge with Philip by his side, but both were safe and sound.

They found Tom Clancy still in his boat; he had almost given up hope that Robin could still be alive. Yet he had waited.

You may imagine what excitement there was when Robin arrived at the Ronaynes' house with their son Philip. The lad looked not one whit changed, nor a day older than when he had last been seen, and the strangest thing was that he could remember nothing about those seven years in the giant's cave. Though his friends had grown to be young men and his parents were older, Philip felt he had never left them.

The Giant's Stairs

Robin was handsomely rewarded for his bravery and Philip grew to be a fine young man. It was noted that he had a magic touch when working with brass and iron, and all who knew his story were sure he had learnt these arts during the seven years he had served the giant Mahon Macmahon, in his cave hidden behind the Giant's Stairs.

The Butterfly that Stamped

This, O my Best Beloved, is a story – a new and wonderful story – a story quite different from the other stories – a story about The Most Wise Sovereign Suleiman-bin-Daoud – Solomon the Son of David.

There are three hundred and fifty-five stories about Suleiman-bin-Daoud; but this is not one of them. It is not the story of the Lapwing who found the Water; or the Hoopoe who shaded Suleiman-bin-Daoud from the heat. It is not the story of the Glass Pavement, or the Ruby with the Crooked Hole, or the Gold Bars of Balkis. It is the story of the Butterfly that Stamped.

Now attend all over again and listen!

Suleiman-bin-Daoud was wise. He understood what the beasts said, what the birds said, what the fishes said, and what the insects said. He understood what the rocks said deep under the earth when they bowed in towards each other and groaned; and he understood what the trees said when they rustled in the middle of the morning. He understood everything, from the bishop on the bench to the hyssop on the wall; and Balkis, his Head Queen, the Most Beautiful Queen Balkis, was nearly as wise as he was.

Suleiman-bin-Daoud was strong. Upon the third finger of his right hand he wore a ring. When he turned it once, Afrits and Djinns came out of the earth to do whatever he told them. When he turned it twice, Fairies came down from the sky to do whatever he told them; and when he turned it three times, the very great angel Azrael of the Sword came dressed as a water-carrier, and told him the news of the three worlds – Above – Below – and Here.

And yet Suleiman-bin-Daoud was not proud. He very seldom showed off, and when he did he was sorry for it. Once he tried to feed all the animals in all the world in one day, but when the food was ready an Animal came out of the deep sea and ate it up in three mouthfuls. Suleiman-bin-Daoud was very surprised and said, 'O Animal, who are you?' And the Animal said, 'O King, live for ever! I am the smallest of thirty thousand brothers, and our home is at the bottom of the sea. We heard that you were going to feed all the animals in all the world, and my brothers sent me to ask when dinner would be ready.' Suleiman-bin-Daoud was more surprised than ever and said, 'O Animal, you have eaten all the dinner that I made ready for all the animals in the world.' And the Animal said, 'O King, live for ever, but do you really call *that* a dinner? Where I come from we each eat twice as much as that between meals.' Then Suleiman-bin-Daoud fell flat on his face and said, 'O Animal! I gave that dinner to show what a great and rich king I was, and not because I really wanted to be kind to the animals. Now I am ashamed, and it serves me right.' Suleiman-bin-Daoud was a really truly wise man, Best Beloved. After that he never forgot that it was silly to show off; and now the real part of my story begins.

He married ever so many wives. He married nine hundred and ninety-nine wives, besides the Most Beautiful Balkis; and they all lived in a great golden palace in the middle of a lovely garden with fountains. He didn't really want nine hundred and ninety-nine wives, but in those days everybody married ever so many wives, and of course the King had to marry ever so many more just to show that he was the King.

Some of the wives were nice, but some were simply horrid, and the horrid ones quarrelled with the nice ones and made them horrid too, and then they would all quarrel with Suleiman-bin-Daoud, and that was horrid for him. But Balkis the Most Beautiful never quarrelled with Suleiman-bin-Daoud. She loved him too much. She sat in her rooms in the Golden Palace, or walked in the Palace garden, and was truly sorry for him.

Of course if he had chosen to turn his ring on his finger and call up the Djinns and the Afrits they would have magicked all those nine hundred and ninety-nine quarrelsome wives into white mules of the desert or greyhounds or pomegranate seeds; but Suleiman-bin-Daoud thought that that would be showing off. So, when they quarrelled too much, he only walked by himself in one part of the beautiful Palace gardens and wished he had never been born.

One day, when they had quarrelled for three weeks – all nine hundred and ninety-nine wives together – Suleiman-bin-Daoud went out for peace and quiet as usual; and among the orange-trees he met Balkis the Most Beautiful, very sorrowful because Suleiman-bin-Daoud was so worried. And she said to him, 'O my Lord and Light of my Eyes, turn the ring upon your finger and show these Queens of Egypt and Mesopotamia and Persia and China that you are the great and terrible King.' But Suleiman-bin-Daoud shook his head and said, 'O my Lady and Delight of my Life, remember the Animal that came out of the sea and made me ashamed before all the animals in all the world because I showed off. Now, if I showed off before these Queens of Persia and Egypt and Abyssinia and China, merely because they worry me, I might be made even more ashamed than I have been.'

And Balkis the Most Beautiful said, 'O my Lord and Treasure of my Soul, what will you do?'

And Suleiman-bin-Daoud said, 'O my Lady and Content of my Heart, I shall continue to endure my fate at the hands of these nine hundred and ninety-nine Queens who vex me with their continual quarrelling.'

So he went on between the lilies and the loquats and the roses and the cannas and the heavy-scented ginger-plants that grew in the garden, till he came to the great camphor-tree that was called the Camphor-Tree of Suleiman-bin-Daoud. But Balkis hid among the tall irises and the spotted bamboos and the red lilies behind the camphor-tree, so as to be near her own true love, Suleiman-bin-Daoud.

Presently, two Butterflies flew under the tree, quarrelling.

Suleiman-bin-Daoud heard one say to the other, 'I wonder at your presumption in talking like this to me. Don't you know that if I stamped with my foot all Suleiman-bin-Daoud's Palace and this garden here would vanish in a clap of thunder?'

Then Suleiman-bin-Daoud forgot his nine hundred and ninety-nine bothersome wives, and laughed, till the camphor-tree shook, at the Butterfly's boast. And he held out his finger and said, 'Little man, come here.'

The Butterfly was dreadfully frightened, but he managed to fly up to the hand of Suleiman-bin-Daoud, and clung there, fanning himself. Suleiman-bin-Daoud bent his head and whispered very softly, 'Little man, you know that all your stamping wouldn't bend one blade of grass. What made you tell that awful fib to your wife? – for doubtless she is your wife.'

The Butterfly looked at Suleiman-bin-Daoud and saw the most wise King's eyes twinkle like stars on a frosty night, and he picked up his courage with both wings, and he put his head on one side and said, 'O King, live for ever! She *is* my wife; and you know what wives are like.'

Suleiman-bin-Daoud smiled in his beard and said, 'Yes, *I* know, little brother.'

'One must keep them in order somehow,' said the Butterfly, 'and she has been quarrelling with me all morning. I said that to quiet her.'

And Suleiman-bin-Daoud said, 'May it quiet her. Go back to your wife, little brother, and let me hear what you say.'

Back flew the Butterfly to his wife, who was all of a twitter behind a leaf, and she said, 'He heard you! Suleiman-bin-Daoud himself heard you!'

'Heard me!' said the Butterfly. 'Of course he did. I meant him to hear me.'

'And what did he say? Oh, what did he say?'

'Well,' said the Butterfly, fanning himself most importantly, 'between you and me, my dear – of course I don't blame him, because his Palace must have cost a great deal and the oranges are just ripening – he asked me not to stamp, and I promised I wouldn't.'

'Gracious!' said his wife, and sat quite quiet; but Suleiman-bin-Daoud laughed till the tears ran down his face at the impudence of the bad little Butterfly.

Balkis the Most Beautiful stood up behind the tree among the red lilies and smiled to herself, for she had heard all this talk. She thought, 'If I am wise I can yet save my Lord from the persecutions of these quarrelsome Queens,' and she held out her finger and whispered softly to the Butterfly's Wife, 'Little woman, come here.'

Up flew the Butterfly's Wife, very frightened, and clung to the Balkis's white hand.

Balkis bent her beautiful head down and whispered, 'Little

woman, do you believe what your husband has just said?'

The Butterfly's Wife looked at Balkis, and saw the Most Beautiful Queen's eyes shining like deep pools with starlight on them, and she picked up her courage with both wings and said, 'O Queen, be lovely for ever! *You* know what men-folk are like.'

And the Queen Balkis, the Wise Balkis of Sheba, put her hand to her lips to hide a smile, and said, 'Little sister, *I* know.'

'They get angry,' said the Butterfly's Wife, fanning herself quickly, 'over nothing at all, but we must humour them, O Queen. They never mean half they say. If it pleases my husband to believe that he can make Suleiman-bin-Daoud's Palace disappear by stamping his foot, I'm sure *I* don't care. He'll forget all about it tomorrow.'

'Little sister,' said Balkis, 'you are quite right; but next time he begins to boast, take him at his word. Ask him to stamp, and see what will happen. *We* know what men-folk are like, don't we? He'll be very much ashamed.'

Away flew the Butterfly's Wife to her husband, and in five minutes they were quarrelling worse than ever.

'Remember!' said the Butterfly. 'Remember what I can do if I stamp my foot.'

'I don't believe you one little bit,' said the Butterfly's Wife. 'I should very much like to see it done. Suppose you stamp now.'

'I promised Suleiman-bin-Daoud that I wouldn't,' said the Butterfly, 'and I don't want to break my promise.'

'It wouldn't matter if you did,' said the wife. 'You couldn't bend a blade of grass with your stamping. I dare you to do it,' she said. 'Stamp! Stamp! Stamp!'

Suleiman-bin-Daoud, sitting under the camphor-tree,

heard every word of this, and he laughed as he had never laughed in his life before. He forgot all about his Queens; he forgot about the Animal that came out of the sea; he forgot about showing off. He just laughed with joy, and Balkis, on the other side of the tree, smiled because her own true love was so joyful.

Presently the Butterfly, very hot and puffy, came whirling back under the shadow of the camphor-tree and said to Suleiman, 'She wants me to stamp! She wants to see what will happen, O Suleiman-bin-Daoud! You know I can't do it, and now she'll never believe a word I say. She'll laugh at me to the end of my days!'

'No, little brother,' said Suleiman-bin-Daoud, 'she will never laugh at you again,' and he turned the ring on his finger – just for the little Butterfly's sake, not for the sake of showing off – and, lo and behold, four huge Djinns came out of the earth!

'Slaves,' said Suleiman-bin-Daoud, 'when this gentleman on my finger' (that was where the impudent Butterfly was sitting) 'stamps his left front forefoot you will make my Palace and these gardens disappear in a clap of thunder. When he stamps again you will bring them back carefully.'

'Now, little brother,' he said, 'go back to your wife and stamp all you've a mind to.'

Away flew the Butterfly to his wife, who was crying, 'I dare you to do it! Stamp! Stamp now! Stamp!' Balkis saw the four vast Djinns stoop down to the four corners of the gardens with the Palace in the middle, and she clapped her hands softly and said, 'At last Suleiman-bin-Daoud will do for the sake of a Butterfly what he ought to have done long ago for his own sake, and the quarrelsome Queens will be frightened!'

Then the Butterfly stamped. The Djinns jerked the Palace

and the gardens a thousand miles into the air: there was a most awful thunder-clap, and everything grew inky black. The Butterfly's Wife fluttered about in the dark, crying, 'Oh, I'll be good! I'm so sorry I spoke! Only bring the gardens back, my dear darling husband, and I'll never contradict again.'

The Butterfly was nearly as frightened as his wife, and Suleiman-bin-Daoud laughed so much that it was several minutes before he found breath enough to whisper to the Butterfly, 'Stamp again, little brother. Give me back my Palace, most great magician.'

'Yes, give him back his Palace,' said the Butterfly's Wife, still flying about in the dark like a moth. 'Give him back his Palace, and don't let's have any more horrid magic.'

'Well, my dear,' said the Butterfly as bravely as he could, 'you see what your nagging has led to. Of course it doesn't make any difference to *me* – I'm used to this kind of thing – but as a favour to you and to Suleiman-bin-Daoud I don't mind putting things right.'

So he stamped once more, and that instant the Djinns let down the Palace and the gardens, without even a bump. The sun shone on the dark-green orange-leaves, the fountains played among the pink Egyptian lilies; the birds went on singing; and the Butterfly's Wife lay on her side under the camphor-tree waggling her wings and panting, 'Oh, I'll be good! I'll be good!'

Suleiman-bin-Daoud could hardly speak for laughing. He leaned back all weak and hiccoughy, and shook his finger at the Butterfly and said, 'O great wizard, what is the sense of returning to me my Palace if at the same time you slay me with mirth?'

Then came a terrible noise, for all the nine hundred and

ninety-nine Queens ran out of the Palace shrieking and shouting and calling for their babies. They hurried down the great
marble steps below the fountain, one hundred abreast, and
the Most Wise Balkis went statelily forward to meet them and
said, 'What is your trouble, O Queens?'

They stood on the marble steps one hundred abreast and
shouted, '*What* is our trouble? We were living peacefully in
our golden Palace, as is our custom, when upon a sudden the
Palace disappeared, and we were left sitting in a thick and
noisome darkness; and it thundered, and Djinns and Afrits
moved about in the darkness! *That* is our trouble, O Head
Queen, and we are most extremely troubled on account of
that trouble, for it was a troublesome trouble, unlike any
trouble we have known.'

Then Balkis the Most Beautiful Queen – Suleiman-bin-
Daoud's Very Best Beloved – Queen that was of Sheba and
Sabie and the Rivers of the Gold of the South – from the
Desert of Zinn to the Towers of Zimbabwe – Balkis, almost as
wise as the Most Wise Suleiman-bin-Daoud himself, said, 'It
is nothing, O Queens! A Butterfly has made complaint against
his wife because she quarrelled with him, and it has pleased
our Lord Suleiman-bin-Daoud to teach her a lesson in low-
speaking and humbleness, for that is counted a virtue among
the wives of the butterflies.'

Then up and spoke an Egyptian Queen – the daughter of a
Pharaoh – and she said, 'Our Palace cannot be plucked up by
the roots like a leek for the sake of a little insect. No! Suleiman-
bin-Daoud must be dead, and what we heard and saw was the
earth thundering and darkening at the news.'

Then Balkis beckoned that bold Queen without looking at
her, and said to her and to the others, 'Come and see.'

They came down the marble steps, one hundred abreast,

41

and beneath his camphor-tree, still weak with laughing, they saw the Most Wise King Suleiman-bin-Daoud rocking back and forth with a Butterfly on either hand, and they heard him say, 'O wife of my brother in the air, remember after this to please your husband in all things, lest he be provoked to stamp his foot again; for he has said that he is used to this Magic, and he is most eminently a great magician – one who steals away the very Palace of Suleiman-bin-Daoud himself. Go in peace, little folk!' And he kissed them on the wings, and they flew away.

Then all the Queens except Balkis – the Most Beautiful and Splendid Balkis, who stood apart smiling – fell flat on their faces, for they said, 'If these things are done when a Butterfly is displeased with his wife, what shall be done to us who have vexed our King with our loud-speaking and open quarrelling through many days?'

Then they put their veils over their heads, and they put their hands over their mouths, and they tiptoed back to the Palace most mousy-quiet.

Then Balkis – the Most Beautiful and Excellent Balkis – went forward through the red lilies into the shade of the camphor-tree and laid her hand upon Suleiman-bin-Daoud's shoulder and said, 'O my Lord and Treasure of my Soul, rejoice, for we have taught the Queens of Egypt and Mesopotamia and Abyssinia and Persia and India and China with a great and a memorable teaching.'

And Suleiman-bin-Daoud, still looking after the Butterflies where they played in the sunlight, said, 'O my Lady and Jewel of my Felicity, when did this happen? For I have been jesting with a Butterfly ever since I came into the garden.' And he told Balkis what he had done.

Balkis – the Tender and Most Lovely Balkis – said, 'O My

Lord and Regent of my Existence, I hid behind the camphor-tree and saw it all. It was I who told the Butterfly to stamp, because I hoped that for the sake of the jest my Lord would make some great Magic and that the Queens would see it and be frightened.' And she told him what the Queens had said and seen and thought.

Then Suleiman-bin-Daoud rose up from his seat under the camphor-tree, and stretched his arms and rejoiced and said, 'O my Lady and Sweetener of my Days, know that if I had made a Magic against my Queens for the sake of pride or anger, as I made that feast for all the animals, I should certainly have been put to shame. But by means of your wisdom I made the Magic for the sake of a jest and for the sake of a little Butterfly, and – behold – it has also delivered me from the vexations of my vexatious wives! Tell me, therefore, O my Lady and Heart of my Heart, how did you come to be so wise?'

And Balkis the Queen, beautiful and tall, looked up into Suleiman-bin-Daoud's eyes and put her head a little on one side, just like the Butterfly, and said, 'First, O my Lord, because I loved you; and secondly, O my Lord, because I know what women-folk are.'

Then they went up to the Palace and lived happily ever afterwards.

But wasn't it clever of Balkis?

Damian and the Dragon

There was a king who had three sons and one daughter. One evening the king said to his sons, 'My lads, when you go to bed tonight you will dream. Remember your dreams, and tell them to me in the morning. And according to your dreams I shall know what sort of lads you are, and shall be able to provide for you fittingly.'

The three princes went to bed, and each of them dreamed a dream. In the morning the king took his seat on his throne, and the princes stood before him to tell their dreams.

Said the eldest, 'I dreamed, O my father, that I stood in a wide place and held out my hands. And in my hands there were cities and farms, and corn lands and pasture lands, and flocks and herds, and horses and carriages, and men servants and women servants.'

Said the king, 'A good dream, and worthy of a prince! Your hands shall be full, even as you dreamed.'

And the king gave his eldest son a great estate, on which there were cities and farms, and corn lands and pasture lands, and flocks and herds, and horses and carriages, and men servants and women servants.

Then the second son spoke, and said, 'I dreamed, O my father, that I held out my hands, even as my brother did, and my hands were full, even as his.'

Said the king, 'What better could a prince dream? Your hands shall be full, even as your brother's.'

44

And he gave this son, also, a great estate.

Then Damian, the youngest son, spoke, and said, 'My father, I tremble for my dream.'

Said the king, 'Yet you must tell it.'

Said Damian, 'I dreamed, O my father, that you brought me a pitcher and a basin, and poured out water for me to wash. And my mother came carrying a towel, and dried my hands.'

The king flew into a rage. 'Insolent rascal!' he cried. 'Do you think yourself greater than the king your father, and greater than the queen your mother, that we should come like servants with water and towels for you to wash your idle hands?'

'I do not think it,' said Damian. 'But so it was in my dream.'

The king sent for the executioner, and said, 'Take Prince Damian for a little walk in the wood, and bring me back his blood-stained shirt.'

The executioner took Damian for a walk, and when they were in the wood, the executioner wept.

Said Damian, 'What ails you?'

'Oh, my prince!' said the executioner. 'The king, your father, has bid me do a thing I cannot do!'

Said Damian, 'I have guessed what that thing is. See now, I give you my sword, and I take off my shirt. I am at your mercy.'

Said the executioner, 'I will turn your sword against myself, for I cannot kill you!'

Damian held out his left hand. 'Cut off my little finger, dip my shirt in the blood, and take it to the king. And I will go whither my fate directs me.'

So the executioner cut off Damian's little finger, and stained the shirt with the blood. And he embraced Damian and wept over him, and then went back to the palace with the bloody shirt to show to the king.

And Damian wandered away, he knew not whither.

He wandered, wandered, for six months. He was ragged, dirty, footsore, and hungry. One evening he came to a great castle.

'Perhaps I may find work here,' he thought. 'Or at least they may give me a crust of bread.'

So he went to the castle and knocked and called. But no one answered.

Then he went into the courtyard. And what did he see? He saw a dragon coming in through the gates, driving before him a flock of a thousand sheep. Damian was frightened. But he plucked up heart when he saw that the dragon had no eyes. And he crept behind a pillar, and watched.

There was a huge pail in the middle of the courtyard, and the dragon squatted down on his scaly legs, and began milking the ewes into the pail. Damian thought, 'If I am to die, at least I will not die of hunger and thirst.' And he took his flask and tiptoed across the courtyard, and filled his flask from the pail, and drank.

The dragon heard the glugging of the milk into the flask. He flung out a huge clawed hand, knocked over two ewes, and said, 'What! Would you drink of your own milk, you cannibals?' Then he went on with his milking. And when the pail was full, he lifted it to his mouth. The milk boiled with the heat of his breath; and the dragon drank it all in one continuous swallow.

And when he had drunk, the dragon drove the sheep into a great barn, and shut the doors on them, feeling with his hands. And then he went into the hall of the castle; and Damian followed him.

The dragon sat in a chair, filled a pipe with seven pounds of tobacco, and began to smoke.

Damian crept behind the chair. 'Father!' he whispered. 'Here is your son!'

Said the dragon, 'Since when have I had a son?'

Said Damian, 'This moment am I born, Father.'

Said the dragon, 'If you are my son, let me feel you.'

Damian stood in front of the chair, and the dragon clawed him all over, but gently, not to hurt him. 'My son,' he said, 'you seem a fine young fellow. If you will be my eyes and help me, I will care for you and love you.'

Said Damian, 'I will be your eyes and help you, my father.'

Said the dragon, 'Then I love you, my son, and I will care for you. You see that I live on milk; but that is not enough for a fine growing lad. Here is a diamond wand. Wave it to the right, and it will bring you a table spread with food. Wave it to the left, and the table will disappear.'

Damian took the wand and waved it to the right. And there before him stood a table spread with all sorts of good things to eat and drink. He ate, and ate, and ate, for he was starving. And when he could eat no more, he waved the wand to the left, and the table disappeared.

'And now,' said Damian to the dragon, 'what can I do to help you?'

He found plenty to do. Every room in the castle was choked with dust and spiders' webs; the dragon had been blind for thirty-two years, and for thirty-two years the broom had stood unused in a corner. So Damian swept and tidied up the rooms, and scoured the big milk-pail, and raked out the ashes on the hearth, and carried in wood, and kept the fire going. All this he did day after day, and the dragon came to love him more and more.

One day, when the dragon was out with the sheep, Damian found a flute on a shelf, and he took it down and began to play a merry tune. And as soon as he played, everything began to dance. The chairs and the tables danced about the floor, and the pots and pans danced on the shelves, and the castle itself danced, jumping up into the air and down again, and waltzing round and round. Still playing, Damian went to the window and looked out, and saw that everything outside was dancing, too: the hills danced, the fields danced, the trees danced, the clouds danced in the sky, the fishes danced in the stream, and the stream waltzed with the meadows, till Damian felt quite giddy with watching it all, and stopped playing.

And then everything was still.

When the dragon came back with the sheep, he was puffing and panting. 'Ah, my son,' he said, 'we have had a merry day, but a rather exhausting one. I don't know what came over me, but I had to dance, and I heard all the sheep dancing, too.'

'Father,' said Damian, 'let me take the sheep to pasture for you tomorrow. It would be a change for me, and you could have a good rest.'

'So I could!' said the dragon. 'So you shall! You may drive the sheep anywhere you will, except to one place. Tell me, do you see a green hill shaped like a pudding-basin, with trees all round the bottom of it, and a little house on the top of it?'

Said Damian, 'I see it.'

Said the dragon, 'Do not go there. Witch-maidens live in that house, and they steal people's eyes. Eh dear, thirty-two years ago I went there myself, and the witch-maidens stole *my* eyes.'

Said Damian, 'It is only mad people who rush into the fire and burn themselves.'

'Then do not be mad, my son,' said the dragon.

But the next morning Damian put the flute in his pocket, and drove the sheep straight to that very hill. For he had never seen a witch-maiden, and he was curious.

The grass on the hill was long and lush, such grass as grew nowhere else in the world. The sheep ate and ate. With his flute in his pocket, Damian climbed up the highest tree he could see, and looked about him. From a window of the little house at the top of the hill a witch-maiden looked out, and saw him.

'Sister, sister!' she cried. 'Here's a treat our luck has sent us! A prince with the brightest of bright eyes to add to our collection!'

The two witch-maidens rushed out of the house and down the hill to catch Damian. But when they got to the tree, Damian played on his flute, and everything began to dance. The hill danced, and the house danced, and the sheep danced, and the trees danced, and the witch-maidens danced with the rest, leaping up and down, up and down. One of them leapt right up into the tree, and was about to seize Damian, when he caught her by the hair, twisted it three times round a branch, and had her hanging there like a bunch of grapes. Then the other witch-maiden made a leap, and all but seized him, but he caught her by the hair also, twisted it three times round a branch, and had her hanging there beside her sister.

'Set us free!' cried the witch-maidens. 'Set us free, and we will do anything you ask!'

Said Damian, 'Restore my father's eyes.'

'That we will,' cried the witch-maidens. 'We will fetch them immediately if you will let us down.'

Said Damian, 'Not so. Tell me where you keep them, and I will fetch them myself.'

Then the witch-maidens told him he must go up to the house, and there in the kitchen he would find two little imps sitting by the fire. But he must be careful not to say, '*Bo!*' or he would frighten them. He must say, '*Chuck! Chuck!*' and pick them up in his arms and fondle them. Then they would be pleased, and he could ask them to give him the dragon's eyes, which were in a box on the mantelshelf, in the shape of two golden apples.

Damian got down from the tree, and went up the hill to the house at the top. Thinks he, 'I don't trust those witch-maidens! I shan't do what they tell me, I shall do just the opposite.' So when he got into the kitchen, and saw the two imps sitting by the fire, instead of saying, '*Chuck! Chuck!*' he called out, '*Bo!*' And both the imps fell into the fire, and hissed and went out like two little drops of water.

'So what would have happened if I had said, "*Chuck! Chuck!*"' thought Damian. 'I suppose they would have stolen *my* eyes and put them in a box!'

He took the box with the two golden apples in it off the mantelshelf, and went down the hill again. And there were the two witch-maidens still hanging from the tree. When they saw him coming with the box under his arm, and his eyes still in his head, they knew their wicked plan had failed. But they smiled, and said, 'Now let us down!' They thought they could take his eyes from him the moment they were free.

But Damian said, 'My father has not got his eyes back in his head yet. When he can see, he shall come and fetch you down himself.'

And he left the witch-maidens hanging, and drove the sheep back to the castle.

The dragon squatted down to milk the ewes. Said he, 'How's this? They are giving twice as much milk as usual!'

And Damian said, 'That is because I can see, and I drive the sheep where the pasture is best.'

So the dragon had two pailfuls of milk to drink that evening. And afterwards, when he sat in his chair to smoke his pipe, Damian said to him, 'Father, would you like this apple?'

He put one of the golden apples in the dragon's claws, and said, 'Do eat it!'

'Nay, my son,' said the dragon. 'I have had my fill of milk, and I don't care for apples. Eat it yourself.'

'I have already eaten more than you can imagine,' said Damian, 'and they are delicious. They are like no other apples in the world for flavour. Do taste just this one!'

'Well, well, if it will please you,' said the dragon. And he took a bite. 'You're right,' he said, 'the apple is delicious!' And he ate it all. Then he leaped out of his chair. 'My son, my son!' he shouted. 'What is this? I can see out of the right side of my head!'

'You will see out of the left side, also, if you will eat this second apple,' said Damian.

So the dragon ate up the second apple, and he was so excited that he nearly choked himself. Now he had two great glowing golden eyes in his head. He pranced about the room, he flung his scaly arms round Damian, he scratched him with his claws, though he did not mean to. 'Oh, my sight, my sight, my precious sight!' he cried. And when Damian told him about the witch-maidens, he rushed out, and pulled them down from the tree, and turned them into vapour with his fiery breath.

When he came back, he gave Damian a ring with thirty-nine keys on it. 'These are the keys of my treasure-chambers,' he said. 'Unlock all the doors. Everything is yours. I will make you my heir, only you will have to wait a little while; for a dragon's life, barring accidents, lasts for ten thousand years. You will be rather old by then, I'm afraid. But in the mean-time – take what you like! Yes, take what you like!'

So Damian unlocked the doors of the thirty-nine rooms, and went into each one in turn, and saw more treasure piled up there than he had thought could be found in the whole world: heaps upon heaps of precious stones, and rooms full of gold and silver.

'But what could I do with all this?' he thought. 'I don't want it.'

So, just to please the dragon, he picked up a ruby and a diamond or two, and put them in his pocket. Then he found a jerkin of cloth and silver, embroidered with lilies and trimmed with pearls, and some silver shoes and pearly-coloured hose. They all fitted him perfectly, so he put them on. And he found a sword of finely tempered steel, with a hilt inlaid with gold, and a scabbard inlaid with diamonds; and he found a golden shirt of chain mail, so strong that there was no piercing it; and yet so light and fine that it could be worn under a jerkin without the wearer himself being conscious of it. These things he took; and he was going back to show them to the dragon, when he noticed a rusty little iron door which he had not yet opened. He tried all the thirty-nine keys, but not one of them would fit the lock. So he went back to the dragon.

'Father,' said he, 'there is yet a fortieth door, and there is no key to it.'

'No, my son; the key to that door is lost,' said the dragon.

Said Damian, 'And what is behind it?'

Said the dragon, 'Just rubbish – old boxes and broken bottles.'

Said Damian, 'I would like to see that rubbish.'

Said the dragon, 'No, no, my son. I told you – the key is lost!'

But Damian didn't believe him. 'There is something behind that door you don't wish me to see, Father,' he said. 'And I am curious. Surely the key of that door is not much to ask in return for your eyes?'

The dragon heaved such a sigh that the whole castle rocked. 'My son, I can refuse you nothing,' he said. 'But if you go into that room, I fear that I shall lose you.'

'Is it so dangerous a place?' said Damian.

'For you, no; but for me, yes,' said the dragon. And he looked fondly at Damian. And tears, big as the palm of your hand, gathered in his golden eyes, and rolled slowly down his scaly cheeks.

Damian was touched to see the dragon weeping, and he said no more just then about the iron door. But though he said nothing, he couldn't get the thought of that door out of his mind; and as the days passed, he spoke of it again, and yet again. Until, one morning, the dragon gave a great sob, took a rusty little key out of his left ear, and gave it to Damian.

'Take it!' he said. 'Unlock that door if you must; but remember that wherever you go my love goes with you.'

'Ah, but I am not going anywhere!' said Damian gaily. 'At least, only just to have a look inside this mysterious door, and come to you again.'

'You will not come to me again,' said the dragon. And he put his scaly arms round Damian and embraced him.

So Damian walked off with the rusty key and unlocked the rusty door, and went through, and found himself in a stable. In the stable was a resplendent mare, with a coat of dazzling silver, and a mane and tail of streaming gold.

'So, my prince, you have come at last!' said the mare. 'Get on my back. We must be away faster than the wind!'

Said Damian, 'But why?'

Said the mare, 'Because you must go home. The king, your father, is in great danger. The foolish man has offered your sister in marriage to any rider who can leap across the great marsh that lies behind the palace. Many have tried to leap the marsh, but all have failed, and perished in its muddy waters. And all the kings who have lost their sons are leagued together, and are raising their armies to destroy your father's kingdom and take his life.'

When Damian heard this, he forgot how badly his father

had treated him; he forgot, too, the dragon's tears and sighs. He paused but a moment to put on the golden shirt of chain mail under his jerkin, and to gird the sword of finely tempered steel at his waist. Then he leaped on the mare's back, rode out of the stable by another door, and galloped away.

The mare went faster than the wind. She had no wings that Damian could see, and yet she was as often rushing through the air as galloping over the ground. In six hours she had covered all the country it had taken Damian six months of his wandering to pass through. But, when they arrived at a village close to the king's palace, she pulled up so suddenly that Damian somersaulted over her head.

Said she, 'Go into yonder butcher's shop, and buy a bladder to put on your head, and the mangy skin of a dead horse to cover up my silver body and my golden mane and tail. Then go into that pawnbroker's, and buy yourself some ragged clothes, that no one may know us, my prince, when we leap the marsh.'

'Are we to leap the marsh, then?' said Damian.

'Yes, my prince.'

'But I cannot marry my own sister!' said Damian.

'Nevertheless, we are to leap the marsh,' said the mare.

So Damian bought the bladder, and the mangy horse skin, and the ragged clothes, and he and the mare went into a wood and disguised themselves – he as a beggar with a bald head, and she as a lame hack. And they came to the marsh behind the palace, where the king and all his court and a great crowd of people had gathered to see the last unfortunate suitor take his leap and sink into the mud. And when the people saw the disguised mare limping along, and the disguised prince sitting on her back, they roared with laughter

55

and shouted, 'Here comes the Bald Beggar! What, Bald Beggar, must you try your luck, too?'

And Damian rode up to the king, and said, 'I am here, your majesty, to leap the marsh.'

The king was in one of his tempers, because he was determined to get his daughter married by this foolish means, and was weary of seeing so many suitors perish. So he stamped his foot and snarled, 'Leap, you dog, leap – and be drowned with the rest!'

Then the mare drew back a few paces, and took a leap, and went sailing over the marsh and came down lightly on the other side, as easily as if she had just jumped over a puddle. And a great roar went up from the crowd: 'Hurr-a-a-ah for the Bald Beggar!'

But the king turned away in fury. 'Whoever calls that fellow my son-in-law shall have his head cut off!' he shouted.

And the crowd hooted with laughter. 'He has leaped the marsh; he *is* your son-in-law!' they yelled.

The king couldn't cut off all their heads, so he stamped back to the palace. He stamped up to the princess, his daughter, and hustled her downstairs. He ordered her to be shut up in a barn, and fed on bread and water, though it wasn't *her* fault, poor girl! But the queen, her mother, went secretly to the barn, and had a comfortable bed and good food taken into it; though she dared not bring her daughter out of the barn.

Then the king heard that the hostile armies were marching against him, so he set off in a fine rage for the battle; and the Bald Beggar went with the king's men on his lame horse. And by and by the mare gave a great stumble, and the Bald Beggar rolled off her back and tumbled into a ditch. The king, who was passing, turned his head aside for very shame, and the soldiers whispered together and said, 'Ah, the king was proud! Therefore God has sent him such a son-in-law as makes him burn with shame to look on!'

But when they had all passed by, the Bald Beggar threw off his disguise, and the mare threw off hers. There they were now – Damian in his golden shirt of chain mail and his jerkin of silver embroidered with pearls, the mare with her silver body and her mane and tail of streaming gold – there they were, galloping after the army to the scene of the battle.

And close to the battlefield, Damian sat down under a tree, and the king saw him, and said, 'Young knight, will you not fight for us?' But Damian answered, 'It is none of my quarrel. I have come here to look on.'

So the battle was joined. The king fought with all the rage that was in him, but he could not make headway against the host of his enemies, and by and by he was surrounded, and like to be taken prisoner. And when Damian saw this, he leaped on to the mare and galloped into the battle. And, with the dragon's sword that nothing could withstand, he sent the enemy flying and rescued the king.

'Ah, my saviour and the deliverer of my land!' cried the king. 'Come, let us go to the palace; and you shall be king and I will be your slave!'

But the mare gave such a leap that she rose high into the air, and vanished with Damian among the clouds.

The foolish king gazed up into the clouds and said, 'It was not a man! It was an angel of God! I must have done some good deed; and in reward God has sent me his angel to deliver me!'

The soldiers were as astonished as the king. But they could not think of any good deed the king had done which deserved such a reward.

So they all rode back to the palace. And when they came to

57

the ditch, there was the Bald Beggar stuck in the mud. And the king, remembering that the Bald Beggar must be his son-in-law, turned his head aside in disgust.

That evening, Damian threw off his disguise, and went in all his glory on his shining mare to visit the princess in the barn. At first she was very startled; but he said, 'I am your youngest brother – surely you remember me?' And she recognized him, and threw her arms round him, and laughed and laughed for joy.

The king heard her laughing. He said, 'The shameless hussy! That Bald Beggar is in the barn making love to her, and she dares to giggle. She shan't live another moment! I am going to put an end to her!'

But the queen caught hold of him and cried, 'In heaven's name, what are you about? Perhaps the poor girl is only laughing for grief!'

So the king put his sword back in its scabbard, and sent a maid-servant to tell the princess to stop laughing. But when the maid-servant went into the barn, and saw Damian in all his glory, she stood and stared at him, and forgot to say anything.

In the barn the laughter and the joyful exclamations and the chattering still went on, and the king, who heard it all, became more and more furious. The queen couldn't hold him. 'I am going to kill the lot of them!' he shouted, and rushed into the barn. But when he saw Damian standing there in all his glory, his fury was changed to delight, and he cried out, 'Ah, my deliverer! Have you deigned to enter the barn? Come, let us go upstairs!'

Said Damian, 'Tomorrow I will come. Tonight I will stay here.'

So the king rushed away to tell the queen that their mighty

deliverer was deigning to pay them a visit in the morning. And he ordered every room in the palace to be adorned with gold and silver hangings, and all the floors to be strewn with sweet-smelling flowers. And in the morning, he went to the barn with his servants, and bade the servants carry Damian on a velvet cushion up into the palace, that his feet might not touch the ground.

In the hall, the tables were spread for a sumptuous feast, and Damian asked if he might wash his hands before he dined. And the king came with a silver ewer and a golden basin, and poured out water for Damian to wash; and the queen came with a towel and dried his hands.

And Damian remembered his dream.

So, after they had feasted, Damian stood up and said he would like to tell them a story, but no one must interrupt.

'No one shall!' shouted the king. 'If anyone does, I will have his head!' And he called the executioner to sit beside him in readiness.

Then Damian began his story: 'Once upon a time there was a king who had three sons, and one night he told them to go to sleep, and in the morning to tell him in turn what each one had dreamed . . .'

'Why,' shouted the king, 'I was the king who did that!'

'Hush, hush, your majesty!' whispered the executioner. 'I should be loath to cut off your royal head.'

So the king clapped his hand before his mouth, and Damian went on with his story. And the king interrupted again and again, until, if he had had fifty heads, he must have forfeited them all.

But Damian only laughed, and went on with his story. And when he came to tell of himself and the executioner in the wood, and about cutting off his little finger and dipping his shirt in the blood, he held out his left hand with the little finger missing.

'I am that prince,' he said. And he turned to the executioner. 'And it was you who saved my life.'

The king was so ashamed that he slipped out of his chair and hid under the table. But Damian laughed and pulled him out, and sat him in his chair again. 'Now we are all happy,' he said, 'and we will let bygones be bygones. But you must reward the executioner with a dukedom.'

'I will do anything you say!' cried the king. 'I will grovel before you! I will give you my throne!'

Said Damian, 'I don't want you to grovel, and I don't want your throne. But I think it would be a good thing if you could control your temper.'

After that, they all lived happily. The king did try to control his temper; and if sometimes it broke out, Damian had only to hold up his left hand with the little finger missing from it, and the king was instantly silent.

Damian hadn't given a thought to the poor old dragon who had been so kind to him. Until one day the gold and silver mare said to him, 'Have you forgotten where you found me?'

Then Damian remembered the dragon, and said, 'Take me to him.'

He leaped on the mare's back, and the mare galloped off with him faster than flying. In six hours they came to the dragon's castle. And there was the dragon in the courtyard, with his great flock of sheep about him. He was milking the ewes, and shedding tears as big as the palm of your hand into the milk-pail.

Damian got down from the mare, and crept up behind the dragon.

'Father!' he whispered. 'Here is your son.'

The dragon leaped up. He was so delighted that he upset the pail and sent the ewes running in all directions.

'My son! My son!' he sobbed, folding Damian in his scaly arms.

'I have brought back your gold and silver mare,' said Damian.

'Keep her!' sobbed the dragon. 'All that I have is yours. Only let her bring you to see me sometimes. Don't forget me again!'

'She shall bring me at every full moon,' said Damian. 'I give you my word.'

And he kept his word.

So the dragon never shed any more tears for grief; but only sometimes he shed them for joy.

Yashka and the Witch

On the edge of a forest, beside a lake, lived a poor woodcutter and his wife. They had no children and this made them very sad. The wife was for ever grieving that she had no baby to rock in the cradle, no baby to sing to and care for.

One fine day her husband went into the forest, chopped a nice round log from a tree and brought it home to his wife.

'Rock that,' he said.

The wife put the log in the cradle and began to rock it and as she rocked she sang,

> Rock-a-bye, rock-a-bye, my little one,
> In my little cradle sleeps my darling son.

She went on rocking in this way for one whole day, and the next, and then on the third day, there in the cradle, she was overjoyed to find not a log but a real live baby boy instead. The parents called their son Yashka and as he grew up he longed for the day when he could go out fishing all by himself, in his *own* little boat, on the lake which he loved so dearly.

On his seventh birthday he said to his father, 'Dear father, would you please make me a boat of gold and a paddle of silver, and when I go fishing on our lake I will bring you back as many fish as ever you may need.' So his father built him a little boat of gold and a paddle of silver to go with it, and every day Yashka would go out in his little golden boat with his fishing rod, and paddle to the middle of the lake, and there he would fish the whole day long till the sun went down. At midday, though, his mother would bring him his dinner. She would come to the lakeside, cup her hands and call:

Yashka and the Witch

Yashka, my son, your work is half done,
Bring me your fish and eat up this dish.

And Yashka would paddle his boat to the lakeside, give his mother the fish he had caught and eat his dinner.

Now the witch, Baba Yaga, the bony one, lived deep in the forest which surrounded the lake. She had heard Yashka's mother call to him, so one day, just before noon, she took a sack and a long hook, made her way to the edge of the lake and called:

Yashka, my son, your work is half done,
Come bring me your fish and eat up this dish.

So Yashka paddled his boat to the shore, thinking it was his mother calling him, and Baba Yaga hooked her long hook to his boat, dragged it to the bank, seized the boy and pushed him into the sack. 'That's the end of your fishing!' she gloated, rubbing her skinny hands. She slung the sack over her shoulder and trudged back to her hut, deep in the forest. But as the sack was very heavy and the climb to her hut was very steep she sat down to rest. She soon dozed off, snoring a most witch-like snore. Yashka managed to crawl out of the sack, filled it with heavy stones and rushed through the forest back to the lake.

When Baba Yaga woke up she picked up the sack again and carried it to her hut. Inside was her daughter, more hideous than Baba Yaga herself. 'There!' said the old crone, 'I've bagged a fine one here,' and she tipped up the sack . . . and out came tumbling all those heavy stones. Baba Yaga flew into a most frightful rage. Stamping and shrieking and brandishing her besom, she yelled, 'I'll show him. He'll not cheat me a second time.' Off she flew in her mortar, beating furiously with her pestle and sweeping her tracks with her besom, back to the lake. In a voice that barely concealed her fury she called:

> *Yashka, my son, your work is half done,*
> *Come bring me your fish and eat up this dish.*

'That's not my mother's voice,' cried Yashka. 'Her voice is not so thick and rough.'

'Not so thick, is it?' muttered the witch. 'I'll soon make it finer, my boy, never you fear!' And off she flew to the blacksmith.

'Blacksmith, blacksmith,' she croaked. 'Forge me a voice, a fine voice, a voice as fine as Yashka's mother's.' The terrified smith set to work. 'Place your tongue on my anvil,' he said, and Baba Yaga stuck out her long, monstrous tongue and the smith flattened it on his anvil. The witch then hurried back to the lake. This time, in a gentle voice, she called:

> *Yashka, my son, your work is half done,*
> *Come bring me your fish and eat of this dish.*

Yashka heard the call and thought it was his mother's. He paddled his boat to the shore. Baba Yaga, hidden in a thicket, quickly sprang out, hooked him in and bundled him into a sack. 'You won't get away this time!' she snarled. She dragged poor Yashka in the sack back to her hut and, kicking the door open, she shouted in triumph to her daughter, 'Heat up the oven quick, my girl.' Then off she swept, while her daughter got everything ready. Yashka hardly dared look at the daughter, so frighteningly ugly was she with her fanged teeth, long hook-like chin and clawing finger-nails. He shuddered, but he kept his wits. The witch-girl brought in a flat shovel. 'Lie down on that,' she shrieked. Yashka lay down on the shovel but he stuck his legs up in the air. 'No, not like

that!' screamed Baba Yaga's daughter. 'I can't get you into the oven with your legs sticking up!' Yashka then dropped his legs over the side of the shovel. 'No, that's no good either!' yelled the daughter.

'Well, you show me how,' said Yashka.

'This is how!' she snarled and she lay down on the shovel to show him. Quick as lightning Yashka pushed the shovel with the witch on it into the oven and closed it tight. Out he rushed from the hut and was just in time to leap on to the branch of a tree and hide among the leaves, as Baba Yaga came back into the hut. She called her daughter, but nobody answered and she realized that the boy had somehow escaped yet again. The old crone went black with rage. She rushed straight out of the hut and made for the tree where he was hiding. Blind with fury, she hacked at the tree with her claws and gouged it with her fanged teeth. She gnawed and scraped till she broke her teeth. But the tree held firm.

More frantic than ever, she rushed to the blacksmith.

'Forge me an axe to chop down that tree,' she screamed. The trembling smith had no choice but to obey, and when the axe was ready Baba Yaga flew back with it to the tree and tried to hew it down. After several mighty blows the tree leaned over, and just as she dealt a final cut the axe struck against a stone so that its blade became chipped and blunt. At that very moment a flock of geese came flying by.

'Geese! Geese!' cried Yashka, 'the bony-legged Baba Yaga is trying to catch me. Please, geese, drop me each a feather so that I can make wings and fly back to my mother and father.'

Feathers came flying down towards him and Yashka made them into wings. Baba Yaga, in a frenzy, chopped so hard that the tree came crashing down on top of her and struck her dead.

Yashka flew home, and the geese followed. He landed on the thatched roof of his cottage and was just in time to hear his mother saying to his father, 'Let us eat to give us strength. Perhaps today we shall find our darling Yashka. Here is some good hot bortsch for you, my dear.'

'And what about some for me?' called Yashka down the chimney.

His parents did not know whether to laugh or cry to see him fly into the cottage with his goose-feather wings. They showed their gratitude to the geese by throwing them lots of the choicest grain and seeds.

As for Yashka, after rejoicing with his parents at his safe homecoming, he went, the following day, in search of his little golden boat. And there it was, just where the witch had left it, with its silver paddle, waiting for Yashka to row it away.

Every day he went fishing on his lake, and caught more than enough fish for them all to live happily to the end of their days.

The Cave of the Cyclops

Long ago a ship was sailing home across the seas to Greece. A great leader, Odysseus, commanded it. He was a small man but he had great cunning.

One dark night the ship dropped anchor off a strange coast. When daylight came the men could see the smoke of distant fires. They could hear the bleating of sheep and goats far off. Sometimes they could even hear the rumble of huge voices.

They could see on shore the mouth of a great cave, overhung with laurel. A wall of stone had been built outside the cave. It made an enclosure where sheep and goats could be shut at night.

Now Odysseus chose twelve of his best men to explore with him. They took food with them and strong wine, and went ashore.

They reached the cave. They found it empty, except for lambs and kids. Someone had penned them there, and someone had left pails and bowls for milking, and someone had made great cheeses and stored them in baskets. Someone used this cave as his home.

The twelve men were afraid. They wanted to take some cheese and some of the kids and lambs and go quickly back to the ship and sail away. But Odysseus would not let them. He wanted to see who was the owner of the cave.

So they waited.

They lit a fire in the cave. They ate a meal.

They waited.

At last, at sunset, they heard footsteps. They heard heavy footsteps coming nearer and nearer. They saw a shadow fall across the mouth of the cave. A huge body blocked out the sunlight from the mouth of the cave.

The owner of the cave came in. He was a giant – a giant and a monster, for he had only one eye in the middle of his forehead. He was a Cyclops.

The Cyclops drove his flock before him into the cave.

A stone lay by the mouth of the cave – a stone so huge that a gang of men with twenty waggons could not have shifted it. The Cyclops picked it up like a pebble.

He set it over the mouth of the cave, blocking it.

Next the Cyclops milked his goats and sheep, filling the pails and bowls.

Then he lit his fire.

And now he caught sight of Odysseus and his men. 'Strangers!' he boomed. 'Who are you, and where do you come from?'

Odysseus answered for them all. 'We are Greeks,' he said, 'and we are sailing home to Greece. We beg you, in the name of the gods, to help us on our way.'

The Cyclops laughed, and said, 'My people care nothing for the gods.'

He said not another word. He reached out with his huge hands and snatched up two of the twelve men, tore them to pieces, and ate them.

Odysseus and the rest of his men looked on in horror.

When the Cyclops had finished, he drank a bowl of milk, and stretched himself out to sleep.

Now Odysseus drew his sword to kill the Cyclops as he slept. Then he thought again. Once the Cyclops was dead, there was no one strong enough to move the door-stone from the mouth of the cave.

They would all be shut in there to die.

So they waited.

In the morning the Cyclops woke and milked his sheep again as usual. Then again he snatched two of Odysseus' men and killed and ate them for his breakfast. Then he gathered his sheep together at the cave-mouth. He moved the door-stone back. He drove the sheep out. He moved the door-stone back again at once.

Odysseus and his men were left shut in the cave. They could hear the bleating of the sheep going away in the distance. They could hear the merry whistling of the Cyclops as he went with them.

By now Odysseus had a plan for revenge and escape. He found a tree-trunk which the Cyclops had set aside to carry as his stick. He told his men to cut it to the length that five men could manage. They they trimmed it smooth, and Odysseus himself sharpened one end to a point. They held this point in the fire to harden it. Then they hid their weapon under the rubbish in the cave.

They waited.

At sunset the Cyclops came home with his flock of sheep. He moved the door-stone to bring them in. Then he moved it back again. He milked his sheep as usual. Then he seized two more of the Greeks and ate his horrible supper.

When he had finished, Odysseus brought him a bowl of wine to drink. It was strong wine, and no water had been added to it.

The Cyclops drank, and smacked his lips. 'More!' he called. 'And tell me your name, stranger. For I, too, can give presents.'

Odysseus filled the bowl a second time, and the Cyclops drank.

'More!' he shouted again. He was half-drunk by now.

Odysseus filled the bowl a third time, and the Cyclops drank.

He was quite drunk by now, and sleepy. He mumbled, 'Your name, stranger.'

Odysseus said, 'My name is Nobody. What gift will you give to Nobody?'

The Cyclops laughed. 'Why, this gift! I will eat Nobody last of all!'

With that the Cyclops toppled over and lay on the floor in the deep sleep of drunkenness.

Odysseus now took the tree-trunk and thrust it deep into the fire, until the point glowed with heat. Then he and four of his men carried it to where the Cyclops lay and drove the point deep into his one eye.

The screams and shouts of the Cyclops brought his giant neighbours running to the cave. They called through the blocked doorway, 'Why do you disturb our sleep with your screaming? Are robbers or murderers attacking you?'

The Cyclops called back: 'Nobody has tricked me! Nobody has attacked me! Nobody has blinded me!'

So his friends answered, 'If nobody has harmed you, all is well.' And they went home.

The cunning Odysseus laughed to himself.

Now the time came for the blinded Cyclops to let his sheep out of the cave as usual. He moved the door-stone and sat by the doorway with his hands stretched out, groping in the air. He meant to catch the Greeks if they tried to escape with the sheep.

But Odysseus had tied the sheep together in threes. Under

each middle sheep he tied one of his men. He himself clung underneath the biggest ram of all.

The Cyclops passed his hands over the woolly backs of the sheep as they left the cave. He never guessed what was underneath them.

Last of all came the biggest ram, with Odysseus clinging underneath him. The Cyclops stroked it as it passed. Now all the sheep were out of the cave.

Once they were clear of the cave, Odysseus dropped from his ram and untied the rest of his men. They hurried to the ship, driving some of the sheep before them. When everyone was aboard, Odysseus shouted back to the Cyclops:

'Cyclops, never again tell your friends that you were blinded by Nobody. Tell them, instead, that the deed was done by Odysseus of Greece.'

Boffy and the
Teacher Eater

Boffy was six years old. He was small and rather thin. Large spectacles covered his pale, serious face. Boffy did not think about tadpoles and chewing-gum and model cars the way other boys did, he wanted more than anything to be an inventor.

'You can't be one until you're grown-up,' said his tall, important-looking father. 'You're not old enough.'

'But I'm a genius,' pointed out Boffy.

'Yes,' said his mother, whose name was Mrs Smith, 'I'm afraid he is.'

She found living with a genius very difficult; geniuses are inclined to think it's tea-time when it's only breakfast-time. And they make complicated arrangements with the biscuits instead of just eating them. And *always* use a long word where a short one would do.

Mr Smith was going to work. He was rushing to catch the underground train. Boffy had made a wonderful vehicle out of empty fruit cans. It hopped on and off pavements, knew when not to bump into lamp-posts without being told, and could even climb over things if necessary, like a great caterpillar.

'Borrow it,' suggested Boffy. 'It will get you there more quickly.'

'No, thank you,' said Mr Smith politely. He preferred the more conventional form of transport.

So Boffy climbed into the fruit-can vehicle himself, and rattled off to town to collect his mother's groceries. He loaded beans into one container, potatoes into another, and secured half a boiled pig to the back. He took longer doing this than he had expected, so when he came to the gas-works he drove straight over it instead of going round it, which saved a lot of time. This greatly surprised Constable Scuffer. But by the time he'd thought what to do about it Boffy was out of sight.

Mrs Smith was glad to have her groceries so quickly. She wanted to get the lunch in the oven early so that she could make a start with her spring-cleaning.

Soon the kitchen was full of buckets and mops and soap and polish and dusters and dishcloths.

'Did you ever see such dust!' she exclaimed. She was red in the face and quite bothered.

'I'll help you,' said Boffy.

'No, thank you,' panted Mrs Smith; she was aghast at the thought of another of Boffy's inventions.

'There must be quicker ways of cleaning a room than this!' Boffy waved his hand at the conglomeration of mops and dusters.

'There is no better way than by getting down on one's hands and knees,' answered his mother, beginning to do just that.

But Boffy was already in his little workshop behind the cabbage patch. He knew exactly what he was going to do because, as I have told you before, he was a genius. In no time at all he had made a large interesting-looking machine. It had a horn at one end, and a plastic sack at the other, and it was held together by a great many rubber tubes.

'What is it?' asked Mrs Smith, as Boffy appeared in the kitchen doorway with the new invention.

74

'It's a Dust Extractor, of course.'

'Well, I don't need it.' His mother was quite firm. 'I've been doing my spring-cleaning this way for a good many years now, and I don't intend to change.'

'Yes, but look how long it takes you.' Before Mrs Smith could stop him, he had switched on the Dust Extractor.

'It works!' cheered Boffy.

I cannot describe the noise that followed – like a percussion band, but noisier! Anyway, it drowned Mrs Smith's screams of 'Stop! Stop!'

Brooms and mops rattled up into the Dust Extractor. A jar of marmalade flew off the table, followed by cups and saucers and the tablecloth. Boffy was delighted. Not *all* his inventions worked. This one was doing fine. He moved it closer to the cooker, which looked exceptionally dusty. At once the pans came to life. Off flew the lids and out popped the potatoes and the runner beans. They slithered and bumped down the tubes of the Dust Extractor. They took the boiling water with them and carried on cooking merrily inside the plastic bag. Last of all the oven door swung open and out shot the half pig.

Mrs Smith was completely DISTRAUGHT.

'You are a DISGRACE!' thundered Boffy's father when he came home for lunch (which was now only a buttered biscuit and a cup of tea). 'You will go straight to your room, without lunch, without afternoon tea, and without supper, and you will *stay* there. And while you are there you will rid your head of all nonsensical ideas.'

'I'm sorry, Father,' apologized Boffy. And he polished his spectacles on his shirt.

It was hard being so awfully clever.

*

For a whole week Boffy behaved like a model boy – more or less. He sat in the garden and counted the bees. When he had counted five hundred and sixty-nine he thought of a number and divided them by it. Then he counted earwigs and subtracted them from the number of leaves on the mulberry-bush.

When the dustbin-lorry arrived he carted his Dust Extractor round to the front garden and offered it to the dustbin-men. At first they did not want to take it, but when they saw how it operated they said, 'Thank you very much. This will make our job a whole lot easier.'

And they took it away.

Mr and Mrs Smith didn't know themselves, it was so quiet around the place. Mrs Smith was worried.

'Do you think you ought to have been *quite* so severe with Boffy?' she wondered.

'Well, perhaps not,' answered her husband. 'But we can't have these frightful inventions of his upsetting the whole household.' (He was a little worried himself.)

'If he could invent something small – like a Boiled-egg Opener or a ... or a ...' But Mrs Smith hadn't any more ideas.

'I'll speak to him,' decided Mr Smith quite kindly. 'Boffy,' he shouted down the garden, 'just be more careful in future, that's all.'

'Yes, Father,' answered Boffy. He was relieved.

The following day was a school day. Boffy was in Class IV – on account of his being so clever, that is. He should have been in Class I, but the teacher in that room couldn't cope with him. He was constantly correcting her, and she didn't like that at all. Mr Grim, however, had been to a university, so he knew one or two things Boffy didn't.

Today he was in a bad mood, because it was the first day back after a holiday. He stared at the class ferociously and made Jenny Jenny cry. He threw a new piece of chalk at Herbert Entwhistle, and made them all write lines.

'He's horrible, HORRIBLE,' wept Jenny Jenny.

'Don't cry, Jenny Jenny,' comforted Boffy. 'I have an idea. Tomorrow you will have nothing to worry about.'

After tea he retired to his shed behind the cabbage patch and he thought, and he banged and he screwed and he fixed. Then he locked up, kissed his parents good night, and went to bed early. His small head was quite worn out.

Next morning Boffy collected his new invention from the shed and set off for school. He carried it a long way round down the back streets, just in case he should meet any of his

important-looking father's important-looking friends. But he met a milkman, and Mr Leggit, the postman, and that was all.

The school cloakroom was packed with children when Boffy appeared in the doorway with his latest invention.

'Oooh, what's that?' asked the children, gathering round.

'It's a Teacher Eater,' explained Boffy.

'Do you mean it actually *eats* teachers?' asked the incredulous children.

'Of course it does,' replied Boffy. 'That's what I've just told you.'

The Teacher Eater was very large. It was a cross between a robot and a dragon. It was constructed chiefly of tin and had a huge jagged jaw like the blade of a saw. On its face, which was simply enormous, Boffy had painted a big pleasant smile. This was not strictly necessary to the functioning of the machine, but Boffy did not want to frighten Jenny Jenny. He had even troubled to glue a black wig on to the Teacher Eater's head.

'Oooh, I like him!' said Jenny Jenny. 'He's *super*, Boffy!'

Boffy kept the Teacher Eater hidden under a pile of coats until after play, then he wheeled it out into Class I. The Teacher Eater trundled across the classroom floor and completely devoured the Infants' teacher.

'Hurray!' cheered the children.

The uproar brought the other teachers racing out of their rooms. They clapped their hands and shouted angry commands. The Teacher Eater didn't like that; it trundled more quickly towards them. A crowd of children skipped and jumped behind it. Suddenly it fancied the Art teacher. She was a delectable mouthful. Her scarlet stockings were the last the children saw of her.

'*Mon dieu!*' gasped the French master. He had no time to say more.

The terrible machine rolled down the corridor hungry for more. It found the Mathematics teacher rather difficult to digest: numbers and question marks shot out of its ears all over the place.

The Teacher Eater was thoroughly enjoying eating teachers. It charged hither and thither gulping them down whole until at last there was not a single one left.

Boffy stored his invention in the games cupboard and locked the door.

'Well, children,' commanded Boffy, 'back to your class-rooms, and I shall be round presently.'

No one contradicted. They did as they were told. They were quite content to look upon Boffy as their new Headmaster.

Boffy retired to the Headmaster's room to draw up a new timetable. It consisted chiefly of games and do-as-you-like lessons. The children played games until they were exhausted. In the do-as-you-like lessons most of them went home.

It was not long before every parent was frantically phoning every other parent. The whole town was ringing and buzzing. Mr and Mrs Smith were thoroughly alarmed and more than a little annoyed with their son.

'You are a DISGRACE!' (again) thundered Mr Smith, 'and you will go straight to your room, without tea, without supper, and without breakfast, and you will *stay* there. And whilst you are there you will consider the damage you have done.'

*

79

The school governors sat up very late that night discussing hard and partaking of refreshments. They were very annoyed indeed. The sort of problems they were used to dealing with were problems like whether to buy a heated fish-tank, or whether to buy new desks for the Infants. They had never had to deal with a problem like the Teacher Eater. It was all extremely irritating. They decided to visit the school at nine o'clock sharp the following morning. Five minutes later they decided that they wouldn't, as the machine which ate teachers might very well turn out to be a School Governor Eater too!

'Highly probable, highly probable,' they muttered wisely.

The next day all the children were in school very early. They wanted to see what Boffy had in store for them. They expected that the morning would be spent in playing games, and the afternoon in painting or in general messing around. But Boffy had been considering the matter. He was enjoying being a Headmaster, and he had decided that his pupils should get down to some serious work. He pinned up a large notice in the hall. It read:

1st lesson—Maths
2nd lesson—Greek
3rd lesson—Chemistry
4th lesson—Lecture in the assembly hall on
          'The Origin of the Species',
          given by Boffy.

                              (signed) Boffy (*Headmaster*)

'What about play-time?' complained Simon Goodbody halfway through the morning.

'You had enough play yesterday,' scolded Boffy sternly.

'But *you're* not working,' persisted Simon sulkily. 'You're just sitting in the Headmaster's room doing nothing.'

'Of course. That's what Headmasters *do*. You will stay in after school and write "I must not be bold" one hundred times.'

Simon hated that. But Boffy sounded so much like a real Headmaster that he was afraid to disobey.

Then a CATASTROPHE happened ... The Dinner Lady did not appear. She had heard all about the dreadful Teacher Eater and was terrified out of her wits. She was afraid it might turn nasty and become a Dinner Lady Eater too. And so the children had no dinner. Jenny Jenny began to cry.

'I'm hungry, Boffy,' she wailed. 'Ever so hungry.'

'So am I,' said Johnny and Kate the twins. And they began to cry also.

Soon the whole school was wailing and moaning.

'And your lessons are too hard,' gulped Jenny Jenny, quite heartbroken, 'and I can't do them.'

'Neither can I,' sobbed all the others together.

'I wish our teacher was back,' sniffled Jenny Jenny, 'I wish she *was*.'

Boffy was cross (and worried and a bit sorry).

'One just can't please some folks,' he grunted.

At that moment, the school door opened and in stamped Mr Smith looking specially important.

'Now then! Now then!' he bellowed. 'This nonsense has gone on quite long enough. Where is the Teacher Eater, Boffy?'

Obediently Boffy unlocked the games cupboard, and there was the Teacher Eater, gleaming in the electric light.

'Right,' said Mr Smith, pulling it out. 'Now *I* have brought along an invention. It's not a new one, and it's not a big one, but it works. Your mother lent it to me.'

It was a tin-opener. Mr Smith started to use it and cut out a large hole in the Teacher Eater's back.

Out rolled the Infants' teacher, then the Art mistress, followed closely by the Maths master, the French master, and one or two others, and finally the Headmaster himself. They sat in a heap on the floor, looking dazed and very crumpled. They could not think where they had been or why. Then they caught sight of the Teacher Eater and remembered. The Headmaster turned very pale indeed, then he said, 'There will be a half-day's holiday today. Good afternoon, children.'

When Mr Smith had driven his son home he said, 'You are a DISGRACE!(third time) and you will go straight to your room –'

'– without tea, without supper, and without breakfast,' finished Boffy for him. 'And I will consider the damage I have done, and I will *never* invent anything again—not until I'm grown-up anyway.'

Then Mr Smith laughed very loudly, and Mrs Smith laughed too. And they thought how lucky they were after all to have a genius in the family.

And all the other mothers and fathers in the town thought how lucky *they* were that they hadn't.

The Necklace of Princess Fiorimonde

Once there lived a King, whose wife was dead, but who had a most beautiful daughter – so beautiful that everyone thought she must be good as well, instead of which the Princess was really very wicked, and practised witchcraft and black magic, which she had learned from an old witch who lived in a hut on the side of a lonely mountain. This old witch was wicked and hideous, and no one but the King's daughter knew that she lived there; but at night, when everyone else was asleep, the Princess, whose name was Fiorimonde, used to visit her by stealth to learn sorcery. It was only the witch's arts which had made Fiorimonde so beautiful that there was no one like her in the world, and in return the Princess helped her with all her tricks, and never told anyone she was there.

The time came when the King began to think he should like his daughter to marry, so he summoned his council and said, 'We have no son to reign after our death, so we had best seek for a suitable prince to marry to our royal daughter and then, when we are too old, he shall be king in our stead.' And all the council said he was very wise, and it would be well for the Princess to marry. So heralds were sent to all neighbouring kings and princes to say that the King would choose a husband for the Princess, who should be king after him. But when Fiorimonde heard this she wept with rage, for she knew quite well that if she had a husband he would find out how she went to visit the old witch, and would stop her practising magic, and then she would lose her beauty.

When night came, and everyone in the palace was fast asleep, the Princess went to her bedroom and softly opened it. Then she took from her pocket a handful of peas and held them out of the window and chirruped low, and there flew down from the roof a small brown bird and sat upon her wrist and began to eat the peas. No sooner had it swallowed them than it began to grow and grow and grow till it was so big that the Princess could not hold it, but let it stand on the window-sill and still it grew and grew and grew till it was as large as an ostrich. Then the Princess climbed out of the window and seated herself on the bird's back, and at once it flew straight away over the tops of the trees till it came to the mountain where the old witch dwelt, and stopped in front of the door of her hut.

The Princess jumped off, and muttered some words through the keyhole, when a croaking voice from within called:

'Why do you come tonight? Have I not told you I wished to be left alone for thirteen nights; why do you disturb me?'

'But I beg of you to let me in,' said the Princess, 'for I am in trouble and want your help.'

'Come in then,' said the voice; and the door flew open and the Princess trod into the hut, in the middle of which, wrapped in a grey cloak which almost hid her, sat the witch. Princess Fiorimonde sat down near her, and told her her story. How the King wished her to marry, and had sent word to the neighbouring princes, that they might make offers for her.

'This is truly bad hearing,' croaked the witch, 'but we shall beat them yet; and must deal with each Prince as he comes. Would you like them to become dogs, to come at your call, or birds, to fly in the air, and sing of your beauty, or will you make them all into beads, the beads of such a necklace as never woman wore before, so that they may rest upon your neck, and you may take them with you always?'

'The necklace! the necklace!' cried the Princess, clapping her hands with joy. 'That will be best of all, to sling them upon a string and wear them around my throat. Little will the courtiers know whence come my new jewels.'

'But this is a dangerous play,' quoth the witch, 'for, unless you are very careful, you yourself may become a bead and hang upon the string with the others, and there you will remain till someone cuts the string, and draws you off.'

'Nay, never fear,' said the Princess, 'I will be careful, only tell me what to do, and I will have great princes and kings to adorn me, and all their greatness shall not help them.'

Then the witch dipped her hand into a black bag which stood on the ground beside her, and drew out a long gold thread.

The ends were joined together, but no one could see the joins, and however much you pulled, it would not break. It would easily go over Fiorimonde's head, and the witch slipped it on her neck, saying:

'Now mind, while this hangs here you are safe enough, but if once you join your fingers around the string you too will meet the fate of your lovers, and hang upon it yourself. As for the kings and princes who would marry you, all you have to do is to make them close their fingers around the chain, and at once they will be strung upon it as bright hard beads, and there they shall remain, till it is cut and they drop off.'

'This is really delightful,' cried the Princess; 'and I am already quite impatient for the first to come that I may try.'

'And now,' said the witch, 'since you are here, and there is

85

yet time, we will have a dance, and I will summon the guests.'
So saying, she took from a corner a drum and a pair of
drumsticks, and going to the door, began to beat upon it. It
made a terrible rattling. In a moment came flying through
the air all sorts of forms. There were little dark elves with long
tails, and goblins who chattered and laughed, and other
witches who rode on broom-sticks. There was one wicked
fairy in the form of a large cat, with bright green eyes, and
another came sliding in like a long shining viper.

Then, when all had arrived, the witch stopped drumming,
and, going to the middle of the hut, stamped on the floor and
a trapdoor opened in the ground. The old witch stepped
through it, and led the way down a narrow dark passage, to a
large underground chamber, and all her strange guests followed, and here they all danced and made merry in a terrible
way, but at first sound of cock-crow all the guests disappeared
with a whiff, and the Princess hastened up the dark passage
again, and out of the hut to where her big bird still waited for
her, and mounting its back she flew home in a trice. Then,
when she had stepped in at her bedroom window, she poured
into a cup from a small black bottle a few drops of magic
water, and gave it to the bird to drink, and as it sipped it grew
smaller, and smaller, till at last it had quite regained its
natural size, and hopped on to the roof as before, and the
Princess shut her window and got into bed and fell asleep, and
no one knew of her strange journey or where she had been.

Next day Fiorimonde declared to her father the King, that
she was quite willing to wed any prince he should fix upon as
a husband for her, at which he was much pleased, and soon
after informed her that a young king was coming from over
the sea to be her husband. He was king of a large rich country
and would take back his bride with him to his home. He was

called King Pierrot. Great preparations were made for his
arrival, and the Princess was decked in her finest array to
greet him, and when he came all the courtiers said, 'This is
truly a proper husband for our beautiful Princess,' for he was
strong and handsome, with black hair and eyes like sloes.
King Pierrot was delighted with Fiorimonde's beauty, and
was happy as the day is long; and all things went merrily till
the evening before the marriage. A great feast was held, at
which the Princess looked lovelier than ever dressed in a red
gown, the colour of the inside of a rose, but she wore no jewels
nor ornaments of any kind, save one shining gold string round
her milk-white throat.

When the feast was done, the Princess stepped from her
golden chair at her father's side, and walked softly into the
garden, and stood under an elm-tree looking at the shining
moon. In a few moments King Pierrot followed her, and stood
beside her, looking at her and wondering at her beauty.

'Tomorrow, then, my sweet Princess, you will be my
Queen, and share all I possess. What gift would you wish me
to give you on our wedding day?'

'I would have a necklace wrought of the finest gold and
jewels to be found, and just the length of this gold cord which
I wear around my throat,' answered Princess Fiorimonde.

'Why do you wear that cord?' asked King Pierrot; 'it has no
jewel nor ornament about it.'

'Nay, but there is no cord like mine in all the world,' cried
Fiorimonde, and her eyes sparkled wickedly as she spoke; 'it is
light as a feather, but stronger than an iron chain. Take it in
both hands and try to break it, that you may see how strong it
is'; and King Pierrot took the cord in both hands to pull it
hard; but no sooner were his fingers closed around it than he

vanished like a puff of smoke, and on the cord appeared a
bright, beautiful bead – so bright and beautiful as was never
bead before – clear as crystal, but shining with all colours –
green, blue, and gold.

Princess Fiorimonde gazed down at it and laughed aloud.

'Aha, my proud lover! are you there?' she cried with wicked
glee; 'my necklace bids fair to beat all others in the world,'
and she caressed the bead with the tips of her soft, white
fingers, but was careful that they did not close round the
string. Then she returned into the banqueting hall, and spoke
to the King.

'Pray, sire,' said she, 'send someone at once to find King
Pierrot, for as he was talking to me a minute ago he suddenly
left me, and I am afraid lest I may have given him offence, or
perhaps he is ill.'

The King desired that the servants should seek for King
Pierrot all over the grounds, and seek him they did, but nowhere was he to be found, and the old King looked offended.

'Doubtless he will be ready tomorrow in time for the wedding,' quoth he, 'but we are not best pleased that he should
treat us in this way.'

Princess Fiorimonde had a little maid called Yolande. She
was a bright-faced girl with merry brown eyes, but she was
not beautiful like Fiorimonde, and she did not love her mistress, for she was afraid of her, and suspected her of her wicked
ways. When she undressed her that night she noticed the gold
cord, and the one bright bead upon it, and as she combed the
Princess's hair she looked over her shoulder into the looking-
glass, and saw how she laughed, and how fondly she looked at
the cord, and caressed the bead, again and again, with her
fingers.

'That is a wonderful bead on your Highness's cord,' said Yolande, looking at its reflection in the mirror; 'surely it must be a bridal gift from King Pierrot.'

'And so it is, little Yolande,' cried Fiorimonde, laughing merrily; 'and the best gift he could give me. But I think one bead alone looks ugly and ungainly; soon I hope I shall have another, and another, and another, all as beautiful as the first.'

Then Yolande shook her head, and said to herself, 'This bodes no good.'

Next morning all was prepared for the marriage, and the Princess was dressed in white satin and pearls with a long white lace veil over her, and a bridal wreath on her head, and she stood waiting among her grandly dressed ladies, who all said that such a beautiful bride had never been seen in the world before. But just as they were preparing to go down to the fine company in the hall, a messenger came in great haste summoning the Princess at once to her father, the King, as he was much perplexed.

'My daughter,' cried he, as Fiorimonde in all her bridal array entered the room where he sat alone, 'what can we do? King Pierrot is nowhere to be found; I fear lest he may have been seized by robbers and basely murdered for his rich clothes, or carried away to some mountain and left there to starve. My soldiers are gone far and wide to seek him – and we shall hear of him ere day is done – but where there is no bridegroom there can be no bridal.'

'Then let it be put off, my father,' cried the Princess, 'and tomorrow we shall know if it is for a wedding or a funeral we must dress'; and she pretended to weep, but even then could hardly keep from laughing.

So the wedding guests went away, and the Princess laid

aside her bridal dress, and all waited anxiously for news of King Pierrot, and no news came. So at last everyone gave him up for dead, and mourned for him, and wondered how he had met his fate.

Princess Fiorimonde put on a black gown, and begged to be allowed to live in seclusion for one month in which to grieve for King Pierrot; but when she was again alone in her bedroom she sat before her looking-glass and laughed till tears ran down her cheeks; and Yolande watched her and trembled when she heard her laughter. She noticed, too, that beneath her black gown, the Princess still wore her gold cord and did not move it night or day.

The month had barely passed away when the King came to his daughter, and announced that another suitor had presented himself, whom he should much like to be her husband. The Princess agreed quite obediently to all her father said; and it was arranged that the marriage should take place. This new prince was called Prince Hildebrandt. He came from a country far north, of which one day he would be king. He was tall and fair and strong with flaxen hair and bright blue eyes. When Princess Fiorimonde saw his portrait she was much pleased, and said, 'By all means let him come, and the sooner the better.' So she put off her black clothes, and again great preparations were made for a wedding; and King Pierrot was quite forgotten.

Prince Hildebrandt came, and with him many fine gentlemen, and they brought beautiful gifts for the bride. The evening of his arrival all went well, and again there was a grand feast, and Fiorimonde looked so beautiful that Prince Hildebrandt was delighted; and this time she did not leave her father's side, but sat by him all the evening.

Early next morning at sunrise, when everyone was still

sleeping, the Princess rose, and dressed herself in a plain white gown, and brushed all her hair over her shoulders, and crept quietly downstairs into the palace gardens; then she walked on till she came beneath the window of Prince Hildebrandt's room, and here she paused and began to sing a little song as sweet and joyous as a lark's. When Prince Hildebrandt heard it he got up and went to the window and looked out to see who sang, and when he saw Fiorimonde standing in the red sunrise-light, which made her hair look gold and her face rosy, he made haste to dress himself and go down to meet her.

'How, my Princess,' cried he, as he stepped into the garden beside her. 'This is indeed great happiness to meet you here so early. Tell me, why do you come out at sunrise to sing by yourself?'

'I come that I may see the colours of the sky – red, blue, and gold,' answered the Princess. 'Look, there are no such colours to be seen anywhere, unless, indeed, it be in this bead which I wear here on my golden cord.'

'What is that bead, and where did it come from?' asked Hildebrandt.

'It came from over the sea, where it shall never return again,' answered the Princess. And again her eyes began to sparkle with eagerness, and she could scarcely conceal her mirth. 'Lift the cord off my neck and look at it near, and tell me if you ever saw one like it.'

Hildebrandt put out his hands and took hold of the cord, but no sooner were his fingers closed around it than he vanished, and a new bright bead was slung next to the first one on Fiorimonde's chain, and this one was even more beautiful than the other.

The Princess gave a long low laugh, quite terrible to hear.

'Oh, my sweet necklace,' cried she, 'how beautiful you are

growing! I think I love you more than anything in the world besides.' Then she went softly back to bed, without anyone hearing her, and fell sound asleep, and slept till Yolande came to tell her it was time for her to get up and dress for the wedding.

The Princess was dressed in gorgeous clothes, and only Yolande noticed that beneath her satin gown, she wore the golden cord, but now there were two beads upon it instead of one. Scarcely was she ready when the King burst into her room in a towering rage.

'My daughter,' cried he, 'there is a plot against us. Lay aside your bridal attire and think no more of Prince Hildebrandt, for he too has disappeared, and is nowhere to be found.'

At this the Princess wept, and entreated that Hildebrandt should be sought for far and near, but she laughed to herself and said, 'Search where you will, yet you shall not find him'; and so again a great search was made, and when no trace of the Prince was found all the palace was in an uproar.

The Princess again put off her bride's dress and clad herself in black and sat alone, and pretended to weep, but Yolande who watched her shook her head, and said, 'More will come and go before the wicked Princess has done her worst.'

A month passed, in which Fiorimonde pretended to mourn for Hildebrandt, then she went to the King and said:

'Sire, I pray that you will not let people say that when any bridegroom comes to marry me, as soon as he has seen me he flees rather than be my husband. I beg that suitors may be summoned from far and near that I may not be left alone unwed.'

The King agreed, and envoys were sent all the world over to bid any who would come and be the husband of Princess

Fiorimonde. And come they did, kings and princes from south and north, east and west – King Adrian, Prince Sigbert, Prince Algar, and many more – but though all went well till the wedding morning, when it was time to go to church, no bridegroom was to be found. The old King was sadly frightened and would fain have given up all hope of finding a husband for the Princess, but now she implored him, with tears in her eyes, not to let her be disgraced in this way. And so suitor after suitor continued to come, and now it was known, far and wide, that whoever came to ask for the hand of Princess Fiorimonde vanished and was seen no more of men. The courtiers were afraid and whispered under their breath, 'It is not all right, it cannot be'; but only Yolande noticed how the beads came upon the golden thread till it was well-nigh covered, yet there always was room for one bead more.

So the years passed, and every year Princess Fiorimonde grew lovelier and lovelier, so that no one who saw her could guess how wicked she was.

In a far off country lived a young prince whose name was Florestan. He had a dear friend named Gervaise, whom he loved better than anyone in the world. Gervaise was tall, and broad, and stout of limb, and he loved Prince Florestan so well, that he would gladly have died to serve him.

It chanced that Prince Florestan saw a portrait of Princess Fiorimonde, and at once swore he would go to her father's court and beg that he might have her for his wife, and Gervaise in vain tried to dissuade him.

'There is an evil fate about the Princess Fiorimonde,' quoth he; 'many have gone to marry her, but where are they now?'

'I don't know or care,' answered Florestan, 'but this is sure,

that I will wed her and return here and bring my bride with
me.'

So he set out for Fiorimonde's house and Gervaise went
with him with a heavy heart.

When they reached the court, the old King received them
and welcomed them warmly, and he said to his courtiers,
'Here is a fine young prince to whom we would gladly see our
daughter married. Let us hope that this time all will be well.'
But now Fiorimonde had grown so bold that she scarcely
tried to conceal her mirth.

'I will gladly marry him tomorrow if he comes to the
church,' she said; 'but if he is not there what can I do?' and she
laughed long and merrily, till those who heard her shuddered.

When the Princess's ladies came to tell her that Prince
Florestan was arrived, she was in the garden, lying on the
marble edge of a fountain, feeding the goldfish who swam in
the water.

'Bid him come to me,' she said, 'for I will not go any more
in state to meet any suitors, neither will I put on grand attire
for them. Let him come and find me as I am, since all find it so
easy to come and go.' So her ladies told the prince that
Fiorimonde waited for him near the fountain.

She did not rise when he came to where she lay, but his
heart bounded with joy, for he had never in his life beheld
such a beautiful woman.

She wore a thin soft white dress, which clung to her lithe
figure. Her beautiful arms and hands were bare, and she
dabbled with them in the water, and played with the fish. Her
great blue eyes were sparkling with mirth, and were so
beautiful that no one noticed the wicked look hid in them;
and on her neck lay the marvellous many-coloured necklace,
which was itself a wonder to behold.

'You have my best greetings, Prince Florestan,' she said. 'And you, too, would be my suitor. Have you thought well of what you would do, since so many princes who have seen me have fled for ever rather than marry me?' and as she spoke she raised her white hand from the water, and held it out to the Prince, who stooped and kissed it, and scarcely knew how to answer her for bewilderment at her great loveliness.

Gervaise followed his master at a short distance, but he was ill at ease and trembled for fear of what should come.

'Come, bid your friend leave us,' said Fiorimonde, looking at Gervaise, 'and sit beside me, and tell me of your home, and why you wish to marry me, and all pleasant things.'

Florestan begged that Gervaise would leave them for a little, and he walked slowly away in a very mournful mood.

He went on down the walks, not heeding where he was going, till he met Yolande, who stood beneath a tree laden with rosy apples, picking the fruit and throwing it into a basket at her feet. He would have passed her in silence, but she stopped him, and said:

'Have you come with the new Prince? Do you love your master?'

'Ay, better than anyone else on the earth,' answered Gervaise. 'Why do you ask?'

'And where is he now?' said Yolande, not heeding Gervaise's question.

'He sits by the fountain with the beautiful Princess,' said Gervaise.

'Then, I hope you have said good-bye to him well, for be assured you shall never see him again,' said Yolande nodding her head.

'Why not, and who are you to talk like this?' asked Gervaise.

'My name is Yolande,' answered she, 'and I am Princess Fiorimonde's maid. Do you not know that Prince Florestan is the eleventh lover who has come to marry her, and one by one they have disappeared, and only I know where they are gone.'

'And where are they gone?' cried Gervaise, 'and why do you not tell the world, and prevent good men being lost like this?'

'Because I fear my mistress,' said Yolande, speaking low and drawing near to him; 'she is a sorceress, and she wears the brave kings and princes who come to woo her, strung upon a cord round her neck. Each one forms the bead of a necklace which she wears, both day and night. I have watched that necklace growing; first it was only an empty gold thread; then came King Pierrot, and when he disappeared the first bead appeared on it. Then came Hildebrandt, and two beads were on the string instead of one; then followed Adrian, Sigbert, and Algar, and Cenred, and Pharamond, and Baldwyn, and Leofric, and Raoul, and all are gone, and ten beads hang upon the string, and tonight there will be eleven, and the eleventh will be your Prince Florestan.'

'If this be so,' cried Gervaise, 'I will never rest till I have plunged my sword into Fiorimonde's heart'; but Yolande shook her head.

'She is a sorceress,' she said, 'and it might be hard to kill her; besides, that might not break the spell and bring back the princes to life. I wish I could show you the necklace, and you might count the beads, and see if I do not speak the truth, but it is always about her neck, both night and day, so it is impossible.'

'Take me to her room tonight when she is asleep, and let me see it there,' said Gervaise.

'Very well, we will try,' said Yolande, 'but you must be very still, and make no noise, for if she wakes, remember it will be worse for us both.'

When night came and all in the palace were fast asleep, Gervaise and Yolande met in the great hall, and Yolande told him that the Princess slumbered soundly.

'So now let us go,' said she, 'and I will show you the necklace on which Fiorimonde wears her lovers strung like beads, though how she transforms them I know not.'

'Stay one instant, Yolande,' said Gervaise, holding her back, as she would have tripped upstairs. 'Perhaps, try how I may, I shall be beaten, and either die or become a bead like those who have come before me. But if I succeed and rid the land of your wicked Princess, what will you promise me for a reward?'

'What would you have?' asked Yolande.

'I would have you say you will be my wife and come back with me to my own land,' said Gervaise.

'That I will promise gladly,' said Yolande, kissing him, 'but we must not speak or think of this till we have cut the cord from Fiorimonde's neck and all her lovers are set free.'

So they went softly up to the Princess's room, Yolande holding a small lantern, which gave only a dim light. There, in her grand bed, lay Princess Fiorimonde. They could just see her by the lantern's light, and she looked so beautiful that Gervaise began to think Yolande spoke falsely when she said she was so wicked.

Her face was calm and sweet as a baby's; her hair fell in ruddy waves on the pillow; her rosy lips smiled, and the little dimples showed in her cheeks; her white soft hands were folded amidst the scented lace and linen of which the bed was made. Gervaise almost forgot to look at the glittering beads hung round her throat, in wondering at her loveliness, but Yolande pulled him by the arm.

'Do not look at her,' she whispered softly, 'since her beauty has cost dear already; look rather at what remains of those who thought her as fair as you do now; see here,' and she pointed with her finger to each bead in turn.

'This was Pierrot, and this Hildebrandt, and these are Adrian, and Sigbert, and Algar, and Cenred, and that is Pharamond, and that Raoul, and last of all here is your own master Prince Florestan. Seek him now where you will and you will not find him, and you shall never see him again till the cord is cut and the charm broken.'

'Of what is the cord made?' whispered Gervaise.

'It is of the finest gold,' she answered. 'Nay, do not you touch her lest she wake. I will show it to you.' And Yolande put down the lantern and softly put out her hands to slip the beads aside, but as she did so, her fingers closed around the golden string, and directly she was gone. Another bead was added to the necklace, and Gervaise was alone with the sleeping Princess. He gazed about him in sore amazement and fear. He dared not call lest Fiorimonde should wake.

'Yolande,' he whispered as loud as he dared, 'Yolande, where are you?' but no Yolande answered.

Then he bent down over the Princess and gazed at the necklace. Another bead was strung upon it next to the one to which Yolande had pointed as Prince Florestan. Again he counted them. 'Eleven before, now there are twelve. Oh hateful Princess! I know now where go the brave kings and princes who came to woo you, and where, too, is my Yolande,' and as he looked at the last bead tears filled his eyes. It was brighter and clearer than the others, and of a warm red hue, like the red dress Yolande had worn. The Princess turned and laughed in her sleep, and at the sound of her laughter Gervaise was filled with horror and loathing. He crept shuddering from the room and all night long sat up alone, plotting how he might defeat Fiorimonde and set Florestan and Yolande free.

Next morning when Fiorimonde dressed she looked at her necklace and counted its beads, but she was much perplexed, for a new bead was added to the string.

'Who can have come and grasped my chain unknown to me?' she said to herself, and she sat and pondered for a long time. At last she broke into weird laughter.

'At any rate, whoever it was is fitly punished,' quoth she. 'My brave necklace, you can take care of yourself, and if anyone tries to steal you they will get their reward, and add to my glory. In truth I may sleep in peace, and fear nothing.'

The day passed away and no one missed Yolande. Towards sunset the rain began to pour in torrents, and there was such a terrible thunderstorm that everyone was frightened. The thunder roared, the lightning gleamed flash after flash, every moment it grew fiercer and fiercer. The sky was so dark that, save for the lightning's light, nothing could be seen, but Princess Fiorimonde loved the thunder and lightning.

She sat in a room high up in one of the towers, clad in a black velvet dress, and she watched the lightning from the window, and laughed at each peal of thunder. In the midst of the storm a stranger, wrapped in a cloak, rode to the palace door, and the ladies ran to tell the Princess that a new prince had come to be her suitor. 'And he will not tell his name,' said they, 'but says he hears that all are bidden to ask for the hand of Princess Fiorimonde, and he too would try his good fortune.'

'Let him come at once,' cried the Princess. 'Be he prince or

knave, what care I? If princes all fly from me it may be better
to marry a peasant.'

So they led the newcomer up to the room where Fiorimonde sat. He was wrapped in a thick cloak, but he flung it
aside as he came in, and showed how rich was his silken
clothing underneath; and so well was he disguised, that Fiorimonde never saw that it was Gervaise, but looked at him and
thought she had never seen him before.

'You are most welcome, stranger prince, who has come
through such lightning and thunder to find me,' said she. 'Is
it true, then, you wish to be my suitor? What have you heard
of me?'

'It is quite true, Princess,' said Gervaise. 'And I have heard
that you are the most beautiful woman in the world.'

'And is that true also?' asked the Princess. 'Look at me now,
and see.'

Gervaise looked at her and in his heart he said, 'It is quite
true, oh wicked Princess! There never was woman as beautiful as you, and never before did I hate a woman as I hate you
now'; but aloud he said,

'No, Princess, that is not true; you are very beautiful, but I
have seen a woman who is fairer than you for all that your
skin looks ivory against your velvet dress, and your hair is like
gold.'

'A woman who is fairer than I?' cried Fiorimonde, and her
breast began to heave and her eyes to sparkle with rage, for
never before had she heard such a thing said. 'Who are you
who dares come and tell me of women more beautiful than I
am?'

'I am a suitor who asks to be your husband, Princess,'
answered Gervaise, 'but still I say I have seen a woman who
was fairer than you.'

'Who is she – where is she?' cried Fiorimonde, who could scarcely contain her anger. 'Bring her here at once that I may see if you speak the truth.'

'What will you give me to bring her to you?' said Gervaise. 'Give me that necklace you wear on your neck, and then I will summon her in an instant'; but Fiorimonde shook her head.

'You have asked,' said she, 'for the only thing from which I cannot part,' and then she bade her maids bring her her jewel-casket, and she drew out diamonds, and rubies and pearls and offered them, all or any, to Gervaise. The lightning shone on them and made them shine and flash but he shook his head.

'No, none of these will do,' quoth he. 'You can see her for the necklace, but for nothing else.'

'Take it off for yourself then,' cried Fiorimonde, who now was so angry that she only wished to be rid of Gervaise in any way.

'No, indeed,' said Gervaise, 'I am no tire-woman, and should not know how to clasp and unclasp it'; and in spite of all Fiorimonde could say or do, he would not touch either her or the magic chain.

At night the storm grew even fiercer, but it did not trouble the Princess. She waited till all were asleep, and then she opened her bedroom window and chirruped softly to the little brown bird, who flew down from the roof at her call. Then she gave him a handful of seeds as before, and he grew and grew and grew till he was as large as an ostrich, and she sat upon his back and flew out through the air, laughing at the lightning and thunder which flashed and roared around her. Away they flew till they came to the old witch's cave, and here they found the witch sitting at her open door catching the lightning to make charms with.

'Welcome, my dear,' croaked she, as Fiorimonde stepped from the bird; 'here is a sight we both love well. And how goes the necklace? – right merrily, I see. Twelve beads already – but what is that twelfth?' and she looked at it closely.

'Nay, that is one thing I want you to tell me,' said Fiorimonde, drying the rain from her golden hair. 'Last night when I slept there were eleven, and this morning there are twelve; and I know not from whence comes the twelfth.'

'It is no suitor,' said the witch, 'but from some young maid that that bead is made. But why should you mind? It looks well with the others.'

'Some young maid,' said the Princess. 'Then, it must be Cicely, Marybel, or Yolande, who would have robbed me of my necklace as I slept. But what care I? The silly wench is punished now, and so may all others be who would do the same.'

'And when will you get the thirteenth bead, and where will he come from?' asked the witch.

'He waits at the palace now,' said Fiorimonde, chuckling. 'And this is why I have to speak to you'; and then she told the witch of the stranger who had come in the storm, and of how he would not touch her necklace, nor take the cord in his hand, and how he said also that he knew a woman fairer than she.

'Beware, Princess, beware,' cried the witch in a warning voice as she listened. 'Why should you heed tales of other women fairer than you? Have I not made you the most beautiful woman in the world, and can any others do more than I? Give no ear to what this stranger says or you shall rue it.' But still the Princess murmured, and said she did not love to hear anyone speak of others as beautiful as she.

'Be warned in time,' cried the witch, 'or you will have cause to repent it. Are you so silly or so vain as to be troubled because a Prince says idly what you know is not true? I tell you do not listen to him, but let him be slung to your chain as soon as may be, and then he will speak no more.' And then they talked together of how Fiorimonde could make Gervaise grasp the fatal string.

Next morning when the sun rose, Gervaise started off into the woods, and there he plucked acorns, and haws, and hips, and strung them on to a string to form a rude necklace. This he hid in his bosom, and then went back to the palace without telling anyone.

When the Princess rose, she dressed herself as beautifully as she could, and braided her golden locks with great care, for this morning she meant her new suitor to meet his fate. After breakfast, she stepped into the garden, where the sun shone brightly and all looked fresh after the storm. Here from the grass she picked up a golden ball and began to play with it.

'Go to our new guest,' cried she to her ladies, 'and ask him to come here and play at ball with me.' So they went, and soon they returned bringing Gervaise with them.

'Good morrow, prince,' cried she. 'Pray, come and try your skill at this game with me; and you,' she said to her ladies, 'do not wait to watch our play, but each go your way and do what pleases you best.' So they all went away, and left her alone with Gervaise.

'Well, prince,' cried she as they began to play, 'what do you think of me by morning light? Yesterday when you came it was so dark with thunder and clouds that you could scarcely see my face, but now that there is bright sunshine pray look well at me, and see if you do not think me as beautiful as any woman on earth,' and she smiled at Gervaise and looked so lovely as she spoke that he scarce knew how to answer her; but he remembered Yolande, and said:

'Doubtless, you are very beautiful; then why should you mind my telling you that I have seen a woman lovelier than you?'

At this the Princess again began to be angry, but she thought of the witch's words and said:

'Then, if you think there is a woman fairer than I, look at my beads, and now that you see their colours in the sun say if you ever saw such jewels before.'

'It is true I have never seen beads like yours, but I have a necklace here, which pleases me better'; and from his pocket he drew the haws and acorns, which he had strung together.

'What is that necklace, and where did you get it? Show it to me!' cried Fiorimonde; but Gervaise held it out of her reach, and said:

'I like my necklace better than yours, Princess; and, believe me, there is no necklace like mine in all the world.'

'Why? Is it a fairy necklace? What does it do? Pray give it to me!' cried Fiorimonde, trembling with anger and curiosity, for she thought, 'Perhaps it has power to make the wearer beautiful; perhaps it was worn by the woman whom he thought more beautiful than I, and that is why she looked so fair.'

'Come, I will make a fair exchange,' said Gervaise. 'Give me your necklace and you shall have mine, and when it is round your throat I will truthfully say that you are the fairest woman in the world; but first I must have your neck-lace.'

'Take it, then,' cried the Princess, who, in her rage and eagerness, forgot all else, and she seized the string of beads to lift it from her neck, but no sooner had she taken it in her

hands than they fell with a rattle to the earth, and Fiorimonde herself was nowhere to be seen. Gervaise bent down
over the necklace as it lay upon the grass, and, with a smile,
counted thirteen beads; and he knew that the thirteenth was
the wicked Princess, who had herself met the evil fate she had
prepared for so many others.

'Oh, clever Princess!' cried he, laughing aloud. 'You are
not so very clever, I think, to be so easily outwitted.' Then he
picked up the necklace on the point of the sword and carried
it, slung thereon, into the council chamber, where sat the
King surrounded by statesmen and courtiers busy with state
affairs.

'Pray, King,' said Gervaise, 'send someone to seek for
Princess Fiorimonde. A moment ago she played with me at
ball in the garden and now she is nowhere to be seen.'

The King desired that servants should seek her Royal
Highness; but they came back saying she was not to be found.

'Then let me see if I cannot bring her to you; but first let
those who have been longer lost than she come and tell their
own tale.' And so saying, Gervaise let the necklace slip from
his sword to the floor, and taking from his breast a sharp
dagger, proceeded to cut the golden thread on which the
beads were strung and as he clave it in two there came a
mighty noise like a clap of thunder.

'Now,' cried he, 'look, and see King Pierrot who was lost,'
and as he spoke he drew from a cord a bead, and King
Pierrot, in his royal clothes, with his sword at his side, stood
before them.

'Treachery!' he cried, but ere he could say more Gervaise
had drawn off another bead, and King Hildebrandt appeared, and after him came Adrian, and Sigbert, and Algar,
and Cenred, and Pharamond, and Raoul, and last of the

princes, Gervaise's own dear master Florestan, and they all denounced Princess Fiorimonde and her wickedness.

'And now,' cried Gervaise, 'here is she who has helped to save you all,' and he drew off the twelfth bead, and there stood Yolande in her red dress; and when he saw her Gervaise flung away his dagger and took her in his arms, and they wept for joy.

The King and all the courtiers sat pale and trembling, unable to speak for fear and shame. At length the King said with a deep groan:

'We owe you deep amends, O noble kings and princes! What punishment do you wish us to prepare for our most guilty daughter?' but here Gervaise stopped him and said:

'Give her no other punishment than what she has chosen for herself. See, here she is, the thirteenth bead upon the string; let no one dare to draw it off, but let this string be hung up where all people can see it and see the one bead, and know the wicked Princess is punished for her sorcery, so it will be a warning to others who would do like her.'

So they lifted the golden thread with great care and hung it up outside the town hall, and there the one bead glittered and gleamed in the sunlight, and all who saw it knew that it was the wicked Princess Fiorimonde, who had justly met her fate.

Then all the kings and princes thanked Gervaise and Yolande and loaded them with presents, and each went to his own land.

And Gervaise married Yolande, and they went back with Prince Florestan to their home, and all lived happily to the end of their lives.

The Fire-Bird

In a certain kingdom, long ago and far away, there lived a mighty and all-powerful Tsar. In the court of this Tsar lived a handsome young archer who was lucky enough to own a very special horse. This horse was so dazzlingly beautiful that people would stop and gaze at it in wonder. It had a long flowing mane, a broad smooth chest and mysteriously gentle eyes. Its hoofs were like polished steel and when it galloped along there was always the beat of thunder in the air and the flash of lightning trailing behind. Most striking of all was its colour, which was that of golden corn, only richer, warmer and silkier. And there was such magic and grace in its movements that everything around was made to seem dull and ordinary.

One day when the young archer was out hunting, his horse happened to kick a large, curved feather, and as it flew up it glittered like flaming fire in the sunlight. And when it came to rest on the ground, the archer saw that the feather was of pure gold. His horse saw that its rider was about to stoop to pick it up, and said: 'Do not pick up that feather, for if you do, you will meet with disaster.' The handsome young archer paused and reflected. Should he take the golden feather or not? If he were to pick it up and take it to the Tsar, he would be richly rewarded, and who would not welcome the Tsar's favours? And so, paying no heed to the warning of his steed, the archer picked up the feather, took it to the palace and presented it to the Tsar as a gift. The Tsar thanked the archer but said to him: 'As you have been so clever as to get a feather from the fire-bird, perhaps you can get the fire-bird itself. If you do not, you will pay with your life.' For the Tsar was a very cruel man. The archer, crestfallen, went back to his magical steed, his eyes filled with tears.

'Why are you weeping, master?' asked the horse.

'The Tsar has commanded that I must obtain the fire-bird itself and bring it to him. This is something no mortal man can do. And if I do not, then I shall lose my life.'

'Did I not warn you, master,' said the horse, 'that if you picked up the feather, disaster would befall you? But never fear, and do not be downcast. Disaster has not yet come. Disaster is still ahead. This is what you must do. Go to the Tsar and ask him to order that a hundred sacks of grain be scattered over this whole field.' The young man went to the palace and humbly requested the Tsar to carry out his horse's bidding.

The next day at dawn the archer led his horse to the field and allowed it to roam around freely while he himself went and hid behind a tree. Suddenly such a mighty wind began to blow through the forests that even the huge oak trees swayed and almost fell to the ground. The waves of the seas rose higher and higher and the whole earth seemed to tremble and quake. All this upheaval was caused by the fire-bird flying from the other end of the world. Immense and majestic, its golden plumage gleaming in the sun, it came swooping down over the field and began to peck at the grain which had been scattered at the Tsar's behest. The magical horse trotted swiftly and quietly up to the fire-bird, trod on its outspread wing with its hoof and pressed it firmly to the ground. The archer now leaped up from behind the tree where he had been hiding, ran swiftly across the field, tied up the fire-bird with a rope, mounted his horse and galloped off with the bird to the

Tsar's palace. The mighty Tsar was filled with rejoicing when he saw the magnificent creature and once more thanked the archer for his services. He conferred on him the title of the Tsar's Most Noble Servant and then proceeded to set him yet another task.

'As you have been clever enough to catch the fire-bird,' he said, 'you shall also get me a bride. In a kingdom at the other end of the world, where the golden sun rises in fiery flames, lives the Princess Vasilissa. That Princess will be my wife. If you bring her back to me I shall reward you with silver and gold, but if you fail you will pay with your life.'

At these words the archer was filled with dismay and he returned to his magical steed with tears in his eyes.

'Why are you weeping, master?' asked the horse, tossing its beautiful mane.

'The Tsar has commanded me to bring him the Princess Vasilissa from the other end of the earth,' replied the archer, 'and I know this is an impossible task.'

'Do not grieve, dear master. Disaster is not yet. Disaster is yet to come,' replied the horse. 'This is what you must do. Go to the Tsar and ask him to give you a tent with a golden canopy, and food and drink for your journey.'

This the archer did. Having packed his tent with the golden canopy, and with a plentiful supply of food and drink, he mounted his magical steed and rode away to the other end of the earth. How long he rode he did not know, but at last he reached the very brink of the world, where the golden sun rose in flames from the sea-waves. And far, far out in the distance he espied a tiny silver boat in which the Princess Vasilissa, plying her golden oars, was tossing gaily along. The archer got off his horse and allowed it to roam over the nearby meadows to graze the fresh grass. He then set up the tent with the golden canopy, laid out his food and drink on a pure white linen cloth and began to eat. He did not have long to wait, for the princess espied the glittering canopy from afar and rowed towards the shore. The tent with its golden canopy excited her wonder and admiration and she made her way towards it.

'Greetings, Princess Vasilissa,' called out the archer. 'Come share my humble meal and drink of this wine that I have brought from a far-away land.' The Princess returned his greeting rather haughtily, but she came into the tent and joined him at his banquet. She drank so freely of the rich red wine that she soon became drowsy and, with a dainty sigh, sank into a deep sleep. She now looked lovelier and more unattainable than ever.

But the archer wasted no time. He summoned his magical steed, which came galloping over to him, eager to carry out his plan. Supporting the Princess with one strong hand as she lay sleeping on his shoulder, the archer swiftly mounted his horse, which sped off, swift as an arrow from a bow, towards the Tsar's palace.

You may well imagine the Tsar's joy and delight when his eyes beheld this most ravishing Princess. He rewarded the archer with limitless gold and silver from the royal exchequer and bestowed upon him the title of Chief Guardsman to the Most High and Mighty Tsar.

The Princess now awoke, and realizing that she was far, far away from her Blue Sea she felt very homesick. She began to weep and grieve and her face lost some of its beauty. However much the Tsar tried to persuade her to fix a date for the wedding, it was all in vain. Princess Vasilissa began to dislike the Tsar, but she disliked the young archer even more for having brought her to the Tsar's palace. She kept thinking of a way of getting her revenge.

One day she said to the Tsar: 'I cannot marry you unless I can wear my bridal dress, and this lies under a great stone at the bottom of the Blue Sea. Let the man who brought me here ride back and bring it.'

The Tsar at once summoned the young archer. 'Ride at once,' he commanded, 'to the other end of the earth, where the golden sun rises in flames. There, at the bottom of the Blue Sea, lies a great stone, and under that stone is hidden the bridal dress of the Princess Vasilissa. Bring that dress here to my palace. The time has come to celebrate the wedding. If you bring me that dress I shall reward you with undreamed-of riches and power, but if you fail to do so you will pay with your head.'

'This time,' thought the young man, 'I cannot escape death,' and when he went to consult with his magical steed there were bitter tears in his eyes.

'Why are you weeping?' asked the noble horse, tossing its magnificent mane.

'The Tsar has commanded me to bring him the Princess Vasilissa's bridal dress, which lies at the bottom of the Blue Sea,' replied the archer, 'and even you must know that this is an impossible task.'

'Did I not warn you,' replied the steed, 'not to pick up the golden feather, for great disaster would befall you. But do not fear, master. This is not yet disaster; disaster is yet to come. Get into the saddle and we shall ride to the Blue Sea.'

For many a day and night they rode until at long last they reached the other end of the earth and they halted by the edge of the Blue Sea. The magical steed saw an enormous crab

crawling on the sand. He trotted up to it and placing his heavy hoof firmly upon it addressed it thus: 'If you do not carry out my bidding you shall die.'

'Do not kill me, I pray you,' pleaded the crab. 'Spare my life and I will do everything you desire.'

Replied the steed: 'In the middle of the Blue Sea, at the very bottom, under a great stone, lies hidden the Princess Vasilissa's bridal dress. Fetch me that dress without delay.'

The crab let out an enormous, weird croak that went rippling over the suface of the Blue Sea and it seemed to rock from end to end. Crabs, big and small, fat and thin – so many you could not even begin to count them – swarmed all over it. The chief crab croaked out an order and all the lesser crabs plunged into the water. Within a few moments they came to the surface dragging a golden casket from the bottom of the Blue Sea. In this casket lay the Princess Vasilissa's bridal dress. Having deposited it on the sandy beach the crabs all swarmed back in the Blue Sea, and the young archer mounted his noble steed and galloped back with the casket to the Tsar's palace. The Princess Vasilissa espied him from her bedroom window and a sadness came over her as she thought of the dangers he had gone through to fetch her bridal dress. Instead of hate she now felt love for the young archer.

The Tsar once again rewarded the archer as he had promised but he was not slow to notice that the Princess Vasilissa's attentions were now turned towards his faithful young servant. And so the Tsar kept urging the Princess to fix a date for the wedding. 'You now have your bridal dress,' he said. 'Why should we tarry any longer?' But the Princess was as shrewd as she was beautiful and she planned a way of getting rid of the cruel Tsar and marrying the intrepid young archer.

One day, when the Tsar had once more asked her to choose the date for the wedding, she said: 'I shall not marry you until the man who brought me here has been punished.'

'And how shall he be punished?' asked the cruel Tsar.

'He must take a bath in a cauldron of boiling water,' replied she.

The Tsar now commanded that a large iron cauldron be filled with boiling water, and that the young archer be bound with ropes and brought before it.

So now the water was steaming and bubbling in the great ugly cauldron and the young archer was led forward. 'Ah me!' he sighed. 'This then is real disaster. Why, oh why, did I pick up the golden feather of the fire-bird! Why did not I obey the warning of my noble steed?' And then, as he thought of his beautiful horse, he decided to make a last request to the Tsar. 'Please, O Mightiest of Kings,' he begged, 'pray permit me, before my death to say farewell to my horse.' The Tsar granted this request and the archer was led to the stable, his eyes filled with tears.

'Why are you weeping, dear master?' asked the horse.

'I have come to bid you farewell,' replied the archer. 'If only I had listened to you I would not now be facing disaster. For the Tsar has ordered that I be flung into a cauldron of boiling water.'

'Do not fear, dear master,' replied his noble steed, 'and do not weep. The Princess Vasilissa has so arranged matters that disaster will not befall you.' And he went on to tell him that the seething waters would do him no harm.

The archer was then led back to the cauldron. The Tsar and the Princess Vasilissa and all the members of the royal court were present; and some say that the Princess was seen to wave her hand over the water and drop something into it. Soldiers seized the young man and flung him into the cauldron. Down he went, once, twice. And twice he came up again and then he leapt out of the cauldron. And he had become so handsome that no pen could do justice to his beauty. The Tsar was amazed at all this and he too wished to become handsome by bathing in the boiling water. Like a fool he plunged in and immediately he was scalded to death.

And the end of this story is that they buried the Tsar, that the young archer married the beautiful Princess Vasilissa and that they lived happily ever after. And for the noble steed they built a splendid golden stable and enclosed a special meadow where he could graze and frolic to his heart's content.

Titus in Trouble

Titus lived in London in a narrow street beside the River Thames. It was a hundred years ago and more. There were sailing ships on the water right at the end of the street. Titus wanted to go to sea, and the master of one of the ships had promised to take him as cabin boy on his next voyage. But a dreadful thing happened.

One day Titus went into Mr Busby's curiosity shop to have a look round. He often went there in search of telescopes and ships in bottles. Mr Busby did not mind, so long as he broke nothing. But today he was unlucky. Reaching up to take hold of an old ship's compass, he lost his balance and stepped back into a table laden with china and glass. A pair of tall vases crashed to the ground and broke in pieces.

Mr Busby was furious.

'I'm sorry, sir,' said Titus, 'I hope they aren't too valuable.'

'They aren't *now*,' said the shopkeeper. 'But before you sent them flying, you clumsy young fool, they were worth every penny of fifteen pounds. I tell you what, though. Seeing you're only a nipper, I'll let you off with ten. Just you run home and bring me the money as soon as you can.'

Titus was too dazed to tell Mr Busby that he hadn't a penny in the world. He said he would get the money as soon as he could, and left the shop. Where was a boy like him to get ten pounds? Some boys are good at mending things. Titus only seemed able to break them. There was nothing for it. He would have to go to work to pay for the broken china.

Until he had done that, he could not think of going to sea.

'I shall get ten shillings a week,' he thought to himself. That was a lot of money in those days. As he strode uphill towards the City, he sang a song he had learnt from his father:

> *Were you ever off Cape Horn*
> *Where it's always fine and warm?*
> *See the lion and the unicorn*
> *Riding on a donkey!*
> *Hey ho! and away we go,*
> *donkey riding, donkey riding,*
> *Hey ho! and away we go,*
> *Riding on a donkey!*

Presently Titus found himself at the door of a great warehouse. He went boldly up to the manager, and said he wanted work.

'Right-o sonny,' said the manager. 'I'll give you seven shillings a week, and you can start straight away.'

So Titus got his first job. It wasn't so bad to begin with, but soon the gloomy factory made him sad, and he wished he was down by the river. The smell of the pickles made him feel sick – for that was what the place was, a pickle factory.

Sometimes he carried the jars to the trolleys, sometimes he stuck the labels on. But whatever he did, by the end of the first week he was wishing he could do something else. Only one thing made him happy – he broke nothing. He dared not.

At twelve o'clock on Saturday, Titus was given his first week's pay, and set off proudly homewards. Then he saw an old woman selling oranges on the quay. The sight of the golden fruit made him thirsty.

'How much?' he asked.

'Tell you what, dearie,' answered the old woman. 'Mind

my basket for ten minutes while I go and get myself a bite to eat, and you can have a couple for nothing.'

Titus sat down by the basket, which was perched on the wall at the edge of the quay. Nobody came to buy oranges and Titus looked at the seagulls circling round the masts. Suddenly a great white sail appeared in the distance. Titus jumped up to get a better view, and as he did so he knocked into the basket. The golden oranges rolled over the edge and bounded and tumbled into the river. Titus clutched at the basket and managed to save it, but most of the oranges had gone.

Just then the woman came back.

'What are you doing, you young demon?' she cried. 'Just look at my beautiful oranges – all gone to feed the fishes!'

Poor Titus had to give her five shillings of his week's money to buy some more fruit. So she gave him one to eat, and he went home slowly and sadly, with hardly enough heart to suck his orange.

Next Monday Titus decided not to go back to the pickle factory. As he wandered along the street, he came to a printer's shop. Here, a printer was making copies of songs and ballad-sheets, to be sold in the streets for a halfpenny or a penny each. As Titus stopped at the open door, he happened to be singing his favourite song:

> *Hey ho! and away we go,*
> *Donkey riding, donkey riding –*

'So you likes a song, does you?' said the printer. 'How'd it be if you was to sing some of these in the streets, and see how many you can sell?'

'I'll try,' said Titus.

'Good,' said the printer. 'Take a bundle of these, and when

you sees folks standing about on the corners or in the market, you starts to sing. I'll give you sixpence a day and a penny extra for every dozen you sell.'

So Titus set off, and presently stopped in an open place and began singing as best he could. He soon learned two or three ballads, and people stopped to listen to his young, clear voice. The passers-by, especially the ladies, were not slow to buy his sheets. Soon he had sold all his stock, so he went back to the printer for more.

For a whole week Titus went his rounds, singing and selling ballads till his throat ached.

At first the weather was fine, but on the last day of the week a storm blew up; just as Titus was turning a corner, a sudden gust of wind and rain caught his bundle of songs and carried them all away, up the street and over the roof-tops. Some went fluttering down into the street, where they were

trampled under foot. Not more than half a dozen could be saved.

The printer took all Titus' wages to pay for the lost ballad-sheets. This made Titus so angry that he went back there no more.

'How shall I ever make ten pounds?' he said to himself. 'I can't even make ten pence.'

The next job Titus got was in a big store where they sold suits for gentlemen, dresses for ladies and stuff for making coats and frocks. Titus was a messenger-boy. He carried parcels up and down stairs, and ran errands for the manager and the assistants. The manager was an important person called Mr Carmichael. He looked down his nose at Titus and at everybody else. He went about as if he hoped to be made Lord Mayor.

One day Titus was sent from the top of the shop to the ground floor with a huge roll of red satin. Just as he came to the top of the stairs, he tripped. Clasping the end of the stuff with one hand and the banisters with the other, he saved himself from falling; but the roll careered away down the long staircase, just as if it were being laid out for the Queen! The assistants and the customers were almost as surprised as Titus. Then something even more extraordinary happened. Mr Carmichael was at that very moment about to go down the stairs. He was speaking importantly to someone behind him. As he put his foot on the top step, he slipped on the satin and fell. He could not save himself, but went slithering right down to the ground floor. A cry of horror went up from the assistants, who had never before seen their manager in such a dreadful situation. But the customers were delighted, and roared with laughter.

Titus did not wait to hear what Mr Carmichael would

say. He took himself out of the building as fast as he could
run.

Titus decided to have one more try at earning some money.

"*Hey ho*! *and away we go*,' he chanted as he strode off towards the big railway station. Surely he could find work
there! When he arrived, an express train was about to start for
Scotland. Porters were pushing barrows to and fro. Pas-
sengers were leaning out of the windows. Friends and rela-
tions were pulling out handkerchiefs. Suddenly the guard
waved his green flag and blew a piercing blast on his whistle.
The engine gave a great roar, and the last door was slammed
shut.

Then a man in a check overcoat ran on to the platform
carrying two huge bags. He almost knocked Titus off his feet.

'Here, boy,' he said. 'Take one of these. Quick, follow me!'

Titus seized the bag that was thrust at him, and the man
wrenched open the door of a compartment just as the train
began to move. He threw the bag he was carrying on to a seat
and grabbed one handle of the other. Titus, still holding on
tight, was hauled into the carriage. A porter slammed the
door.

'I've got to get out!' shouted Titus.

'Too late!' called the porter.

Titus was in the carriage being taken away faster and faster
every moment.

'Sorry, boy,' said the man in the check coat. 'Should have
let go, you know. Only thing to do is wait till we get to a
station. Then you can take the next train back to London.'

On and on they went into the green countryside. Presently
the train stopped. They had come to a level-crossing, and the
gates were shut. A donkey pulling a cartload of vegetables
was in the very middle of the track, and refused to move. So

the man at the level-crossing had had to signal the train to halt.

'Now's your chance,' said the man in the check coat. 'Hop out here. Get back home as best you can. Here's five shillings for you. Dash my whiskers, what a lark!'

He opened the door and Titus jumped down and made for the road. He had no idea where he was, but he could see the roofs of houses and a church spire in the distance.

Soon he came to a big house at the end of a drive. A huge van was drawn up in front of it, and Titus could see that men were carrying furniture out and stowing it in the van. Two great horses were in the shafts, quietly munching from their nosebags. Titus felt hungry. He went boldly up the steps of the house, and was going to ring the bell when a lady came out carrying a bird-cage with a canary in it. She was crying and dabbing her eyes with a handkerchief.

'Ruined!' she said. 'Quite, quite ruined! Yet they must be somewhere! They must, they must.'

'Emmeline, Emmeline,' said a kind-looking gentleman who had come up behind her, carrying a set of croquet hoops and six mallets, 'don't take on so, my dear. We've looked everywhere. There's nothing more to be done. Let us make the best of things.'

'Oh Augustus,' wailed the lady, 'to think it should come to this! If only our aunt had told us where she hid them. But she was always a dark horse, and now she no longer lives to tell us.'

Titus couldn't imagine what was going on. He only knew that he was hungry.

'Please,' he said, 'if you would give me something to eat, perhaps I could find them – whatever they are that this dark horse has hidden.'

'My boy,' said the gentleman, 'I fear you can do nothing, but by all means have something to eat – that is, if there is anything. My sister and I, as you see, are moving house. Our furniture is going to be sold, and we shall have to live in shabby seaside lodgings. We have had to give up this beautiful house, all because our aunt died without telling us what she did with the family jewels.'

'I expect she sold them,' said Emmeline. 'But what is that to you, boy? Come into the house, and I will find you some food. Afterwards, perhaps you'll help us carry our things to this pantechnicon.'

Titus was given some bread and cheese, a few grapes and a glass of milk. Then he helped to take things out to the van.

It was a sad sight, all the fine furniture and carpets being packed away to be carted off and sold. Titus began to feel as sad as the poor lady and gentleman.

'Here, my lad,' said one of the removal men, 'give us a hand with this.'

He was holding one end of a chest of drawers. Titus lifted the other end, and followed the man down the steps. He couldn't see where he was going, but managed to reach the bottom without falling. The man climbed on to the tail of the van, still holding the chest. He called to Titus to steady it below, but alas! Titus could hold it no longer. The chest toppled backwards and crashed on to the ground.

'Now you've gone and done it,' said the man.

At the sound of the crash, the kind gentleman and his sister ran down the steps. Titus knelt on the ground and tried to raise the fallen chest. It was badly broken. Then he saw something on the stones. Quickly he picked it up. It was a package wrapped in tissue-paper, which had been burst open. Titus lifted out something bright and shining. It was a diamond necklace! Inside the package were more jewels – rubies, pearls, and other precious stones. The crash must have broken open a false bottom in one of the drawers, and the family treasures were at last revealed.

'Oh, what a wonderful thing!' cried the gentleman, pressing the jewels into Emmeline's trembling hands. 'What a happy accident! My dear boy, come inside and have some more bread and cheese. Have some champagne! Have anything there is!'

There is little more to tell. Everyone went into the house – Augustus and Emmeline, Titus and the removal men – and as splendid a feast was provided as was possible in the circumstances. Afterwards the men took all the furniture back into the house. The lady and gentleman, their fortunes restored, gave Titus fifteen pounds as a reward for his happy accident.

Titus was so pleased that he hardly knew what to say, but he thanked them warmly, and everyone said good-bye amid laughter and tears of joy. A cab took Titus to the station, where he bought a ticket for London. He was on his way back to where the big ships lay peacefully at anchor in the still water of the River Thames. The handsome reward was safely tucked away in his inside pocket.

'Now I'll be able to pay back the ten pounds I owe for breaking those vases,' he said to himself. 'After that, it's off to sea I go!'

And sitting back in his corner seat, Titus began to sing joyfully to himself:

> *Were you ever in Cardiff Bay*
> *Where the folks all shout Hooray!*
> *Here comes Jack with his three months' pay,*
> *Riding on a donkey!*

Titus in Trouble

Hey ho! and away we go,
*   Donkey riding, donkey riding,*
Hey ho! and away we go,
*   Riding on a donkey!*

The Rabbit Makes
a Match

Ableegumooch the rabbit is a sociable creature, a little boast-ful perhaps, but kind-hearted. So, when he saw his friend Keoonik the otter looking miserable, he wanted to know at once what was the matter and was there anything he could do. Well, it turned out that what the otter wanted was to get married. He wanted to marry Nesoowa, the daughter of Pipsolk; and the girl-otter was willing, but her father was not.

'Why not?' asked the rabbit, eyeing his friend. 'You may not be the handsomest fellow in the world, Keoonik (otters can't compare with rabbits in looks), or the smartest (the rabbits are that), but you're honest and good-tempered and I daresay you'd provide quite a good living for a wife. Did you try anointing Pipsolk's head with bear grease?' This was the Indian way of asking if Keoonik had tried flattery on the girl's father.

'It wasn't any good,' said Keoonik. 'He thinks so well of himself already, nothing I could say would please him.'

'How about a gift to sweeten his opinion?'

'No good. It isn't meat or presents he cares for – it's breeding and ancestors, and I haven't got any according to him.' Keoonik added glumly – 'I'm just an ordinary everyday kind of otter, not good enough for his daughter.'

'Ah, Keoonik,' sighed the rabbit, 'there are many like Pipsolk, full of silly pride. (Pride – that's the one thing rabbits haven't.) Look, my friend, since I am known everywhere as the wittiest and most persuasive Wabanaki in Glooscap's world,* wouldn't you like me to have a talk with Pipsolk?'

'What sort of talk?' asked Keoonik.

'I could tell him what a good fellow you really are and how much better it would be to have a decent son-in-law with no relatives than a bad one with too many!'

'Tell him I'm very fond of Nesoowa, and would try to make her happy.'

'I'll tell him,' said the rabbit, and off he went.

Ableegumooch found Pipsolk and his numerous family sliding happily down a muddy slope near their home on the lake. This is a favourite pastime of otters.

'Step over here, will you, Pipsolk,' called the rabbit from a drier spot up the bank. 'I'd like to talk with you about Nesoowa.'

Pipsolk excused himself from his family and stepped over.

'What about Nesoowa?'

'Isn't it time she was married?' queried Ableegumooch, 'to a kind and hard-working husband? I don't know if it's occurred to you, but a good husband doesn't grow on blueberry bushes. And remember, with Nesoowa off your hands, you will have fewer mouths to feed.'

'Very true,' agreed Pipsolk, 'but a man must do the best he can for his daughter. What kind of father would I be if I passed her over to the first common sort who came along? Tell me, Ableegumooch, who were your people?'

'Eh?'

'Your ancestors. Were they important? Were they well-bred?'

* The Wabanaki were Indians living in what is now eastern Canada, and Glooscap was their creator.

The rabbit stuck out his chest.

'Pipsolk,' he said complacently, 'my family is one of the best. I have a long and noble ancestry, with notables on every branch of the family tree since the days before the light of the sun.'

'H'mm,' Pipsolk nodded thoughtfully. 'Can you show proof of your aristocratic background?'

'Certainly. Haven't you noticed how I always wear white in the winter time? That's the fashion of the aristocracy.'

'Really? I didn't know that. But what about your split lip, Ableegumooch? It doesn't indicate anything common, does it?'

'On the contrary, it's a sign of breeding. In my circles we always eat with knives, which is the polite way of feeding. One day my knife slipped, which is how my lip was damaged.'

'But why is it your mouth and your whiskers always keep moving even when you're still? Is that high style too?'

'Of course. You see, it's because I'm always meditating and planning great affairs. I talk to myself rather than to anyone of lesser quality. That's the way we gentlemen are!'

'I see. One more question. Why do you always hop? Why don't you walk like other people?'

'All my aristocratic forebears had a gait of their own,' the rabbit explained loftily. 'We gentle folk don't run like the vulgar.'

'I'd no idea you were so well-bred, Ableegumooch,' said Pipsolk. 'Very well. You may have her.'

The rabbit had opened his mouth to say something more about his aristocratic forebears, but now he closed it.

'I don't as a rule approve of marrying outside the tribe, but circumstances alter cases. Welcome, son-in-law.'

The Rabbit Makes a Match

Ableegumooch felt as though he had accidentally walked under an icy waterfall. He – to be married – and to an otter-girl! The rabbit had never even thought of getting married. He opened his lips to say so, and hesitated, his whiskers twitching. Pipsolk was a man one didn't offend if one could help it. Many of his kind had a short way with rabbits! Moreover, the thought of marriage was rather pleasant, once one began to think about it. A pretty girl adds a nice touch to a wigwam. Besides, his grandmother was getting old and would be glad of help in the lodge.

He thought briefly of Keoonik, and worded an explanation silently in his mind. 'I'm sorry, friend, but I didn't plan it this way, you know. I don't see how I can get out of it. Can I help it if Nesoowa's father wants the best for his daughter? You'll understand, I'm sure.'

That night, Pipsolk invited all his relatives and friends to a feast and announced the engagement of Nesoowa to the well-known and aristocratic Ableegumooch, the marriage to take place at the end of the usual probationary period. It was customary among the Wabanaki of that time for a young man to provide for the family of his future bride for one year to show that he was capable of getting food and necessities for a wife and family. Keoonik was of course among the guests and hearing the dreadful news, he could hardly believe his ears. He gave his faithless friend a long bitter look as he left the party, and it quite shrivelled Ableegumooch for the moment.

The rabbit tried to find excuses for himself. 'It wasn't my fault. It's too late now, anyway, to back down.'

So he set up a lodge near Pipsolk's and brought over his grandmother, who complained bitterly at having to move to such a damp place near all those noisy otters, but the rabbit paid no attention. His mind was wholly occupied with the problem of feeding those otters. He knew it would be different from feeding himself and his grandmother. Rabbits live in meadows and forest undergrowth and are satisfied with herbs and grasses and tender twigs. Otters, on the other hand, live in or near water and like fish and frogs and salamanders for dinner. If Ableegumooch was to keep those otters fed, he must learn to be at home in the water, and a rabbit is not the best in the world when it comes to swimming. In fact, to be plain about it, of all swimmers and divers the rabbit is the very worst.

'Can you swim?' asked the young otters with interest.

'Well – not yet,' said Ableegumooch, adding cheerfully, 'but I can learn.' Ableegumooch was always willing to try.

He put his nose to the water. It smelled dank and weedy, not at all nice. He dipped one toe in the water to test its temperature – ugh, cold! He pulled his toe out again. After a good deal of sighing and dipping in and dipping out, the rabbit finally got himself into the water chest-deep and began to move his front paws in an awkward swimming motion. The watching otters nudged each other and chuckled. Then the rabbit tried to let go with his back feet, but sank at once and had to scramble in a panic to find solid ground again.

Nevertheless he kept trying, and after a whole day of failing and trying again, he managed to move a few strokes from shore, and all the otters applauded. Ableegumooch felt quite proud of himself, though he couldn't understand why the otters laughed even as they cheered.

Next he must learn to fish, they said.

'Fish? Well, I can try.'

Pipsolk was already fretting about the fact that it was long past his usual dinner time.

'Patience,' said the rabbit, trying to recall how otters fished. They dived first. Yes, that was the hard part. It meant ducking one's head right under the water. Never mind, if an otter could do it, so could a rabbit. And he ducked his head in the manner of otters and muskrats, hoisting his other end high up in the air so the little round tail would follow him down under the waves. Once upside down, with water in his nose and his ears and his eyes, the rabbit thought only of getting up to the surface again. He came up choking and spluttering, and oh didn't the air taste good!

'This way of fishing,' he decided, 'is not for me. Now, let me see, how do the bears go about it? I think they catch fish by just scooping them out of the water. I can do that, surely.' So, standing in the water up to his chin, Ableegumooch reached for a leaping frog, made a swipe at a devil's-darning-needle, grabbed a trout flashing by – and missed all three, to the vast merriment of the otter family. Still the rabbit kept trying. He saw a fat insect alight on the branch of an Indian Pear Tree and at the same time a salmon swam into view. Trying to grab both at the same time, Ableegumooch stepped off into the deep water and sank. Down he went and at the very bottom his long hind foot caught in a pile of brush. There he was held fast. In a dreadful panic, he kicked and twisted, trying to get free. As he fought, a brown shape flashed past him under water, turned and came back. It was Keoonik!

Seeing his guilt clearly for the first time, Ableegumooch was sure the otter had come to take his revenge. Well, thought the rabbit, I suppose I deserve to die, but I'm not going to if I can help it – certainly not to please Keoonik! So he braced himself for one last effort, and at the same time his foot was miraculously freed. He shot up to the surface, more than half-drowned, where Keoonik grabbed him and pushed him in no gentle fashion to the shore.

'False friend! Traitor!' growled the otter. 'I ought to have left you there to perish!'

'Why didn't you?' gasped the rabbit, still coughing up water.

'Because drowning's too good for you,' Keoonik grinned. 'I'm waiting to see what Pipsolk does when he finds out he and his family must go hungry to bed tonight! Ah well – you'll make a good substitute, Ableegumooch. We otters are very fond of rabbit stew.'

'I'm sorry I spoiled things for you with Nesoowa.'

'You didn't,' laughed the otter. 'Nesoowa says she will run away with me rather than marry you.' Keoonik glanced hurriedly over his shoulder. 'Here comes Pipsolk now, and he looks hungry! You'd better start running!'

After one look at Pipsolk's face, Ableegumooch would have been glad to take Keoonik's advice, but he couldn't. He was still too weak and breathless to run anywhere – and in such a strait, as usual, he thought of the Great Chief and whispered a plea for help.

Suddenly Glooscap – who comes as the wind comes and no man knows how – stood between Ableegumooch and the wrathful otter.

'Boasting again, Ableegumooch,' said the Great Chief, who probably loved the rabbit best of all his creatures, 'and see where it's got you!'

'I'm sorry to bother you, Master,' the rabbit apologized. 'It was sink or swim – and I've already tried swimming!'

Glooscap shook his head in despair, trying not to smile. He turned to the otter, who was now looking innocent, as if rabbit stew had never entered his mind.

'Pipsolk, I want you to forget all about breeding and background and such nonsense and just tell Ableegumooch frankly what you think of him as a son-in-law.'

Pipsolk turned to the rabbit.

'The fact is, Ableegumooch, you may be good enough in your way, but your breeding and ancestors won't fill my children's mouths. You'll never do as a husband for my daughter. She would soon starve. Indeed, after experiencing your kind of son-in-law, I can see more virtue in Keoonik's sort. I believe if Nesoowa is willing, I shall give him a trial after all.'

'There!' cried Ableegumooch. 'I told you I'd help you, Keoonik.' But the otter had rushed away to find Nesoowa and tell her the good news.

Glooscap gave his rabbit a severe look. 'I hope you have learned something from all this, Ableegumooch.'

'Oh, I have,' cried the rabbit. 'I know now I'm not cut out for swimming and fishing. From now on, I shall be satisfied just to be what I am, the handsomest, the cleverest, and best-bred rabbit in the world! And' – as an afterthought – 'the best matchmaker!'

Whereupon to the rabbit's surprise Glooscap began to laugh, and he laughed so hard that all the trees bent with the gust of his laughter, and Ableegumooch had to cling to the Master's leg to keep from being blown away.

And there, *kespeadooksit*,* our tale ends.

* This means 'the story ends'.

The Wicked
Lord Chamberlain

If you had been living in Rome about two thousand years ago
and happened to be sitting in the woods outside the city, you
might have witnessed a strange sight. You would have seen a
very proud-looking man riding along on horseback, muttering to himself and suddenly disappearing down a pit.

This man was the Lord Chamberlain, an important official
at the Emperor's court. His name was Marcus. He himself
had ordered that pit, and many others, to be dug in the woods
in order to catch wild beasts as they roamed about. Now
Marcus himself had fallen into the pit, together with his
horse. But they were not the only ones down there. Oh no! A
monkey, a snake and a lion had already fallen in that same
morning. Marcus roared out in terror, and luckily for him a
poor woodcutter named Lucius happened to hear him and
came to see what was happening. He stopped just on the
brink of the pit and peeped warily down.

'Get me out quickly! Can't you see my life is in danger?'
cried Marcus. 'I'm rich and I will pay you anything you like.'

'Your Excellency,' said Lucius, 'I'll help you if I can, but I
shall need a long rope and I'll have to go into the city to get
one. And that will take time. And during that time I shall not
be able to chop any wood. And if I have no wood, I'll have
none to sell. And if I don't sell any wood, my good wife and I
will have no money to buy food.'

'But if you get me out of this pit I'll make you very rich.

You won't need to chop wood any more,' pleaded Marcus.

So Lucius went off into the city, got hold of some rope and returned quickly to the pit. He let the rope down and told Marcus to tie it round his waist. But before the Lord Chamberlain even had time to get hold of it, the lion sprang forward and used the rope to scramble up the side of the pit and escape. It ran off into the woods and disappeared. Marcus now tried again, but this time the monkey jumped over Marcus's head, scrambled up and ran away among the trees. Marcus tried a third time. But now the snake twisted itself round the rope and Lucius, thinking it was Marcus tugging at the rope, pulled it up. When it got to the top, the snake slithered swiftly away and vanished into the undergrowth.

'I'm still here,' bawled the Lord Chamberlain. 'Let the rope down again and get me out of here quickly, I beg you.'

At long last Lucius managed to pull him safely out. And then the two of them, Lucius and the Lord Chamberlain together, somehow succeeded in getting the rope round the horse's middle and pulling him out as well. But it was a hard struggle, I can tell you.

Then what do you think happened? As soon as he was safely at the top with his horse, Marcus rode back to the Emperor's Court without so much as a word of thanks to Lucius.

When the woodcutter got home and told his wife of the day's happenings, she was, of course, disappointed that there was no firewood to sell but overjoyed at the news of the great reward her husband was going to receive from the Lord Chamberlain.

Next day Lucius set out for the Court. He asked one of the flunkeys at the gates if he could see Marcus. The flunkey sent a messenger to find out, but he soon returned saying that Marcus knew nothing at all about Lucius; he had never heard of him and said that he must be telling a pack of lies. Furthermore he ordered Lucius to be given a good whipping and sent back where he came from. Lucius was so sore as a result of this that his poor wife had to come along to the Court with their donkey to take Lucius back home and put him to bed.

After a few days, however, he went back to his woodcutting and firewood-selling. One morning he saw ten donkeys coming towards him, all laden with heavy packs. Behind them was a lion and Lucius recognized it as the one he had pulled out of the pit. The lion nodded its head and waved its paw in the direction of Lucius's cottage. Lucius, slightly dazed by all this, led it to the cottage, where the lion, by further clever paw-signs, made it clear that the donkeys and the packs were now to belong to Lucius. Being a very honest man, Lucius led the donkeys round the village, inquiring whether anyone had lost them. He even put 'LOST' notices in various shops. But nobody came to reclaim them. So Lucius opened the packs and to his great delight found they were all filled with gold. His wife shared his joy, of course, but she still made him go to work the following morning. In all the excitement, however, Lucius forgot to take his axe with him. He was just about to turn back when a monkey appeared in front of him – the very monkey Lucius had helped out of the pit. Using its teeth and claws it began to break good, solid pieces of wood from the trees and went on doing so until dusk, so that Lucius, even without his axe, had a plentiful supply of firewood to take back home.

And what do you think happened the next day? Well, of course, he met the snake he had rescued from the pit. It came slithering towards him with a coloured stone in its mouth,

dropped it at Lucius's feet and then vanished. It was a most beautiful stone, glittering and gleaming and sparkling with the brightest tints and hues. Lucius took the stone to a man who knew all about such matters. 'Ah,' he said in great amazement, holding it up to the light, 'this stone will bring the greatest good luck to its owner. I am prepared to offer you any sum of money you care to ask for it.' But Lucius, sensible man that he was, refused this tempting offer.

The news of the precious stone soon reached the Court and Lucius was summoned to appear before the Emperor. 'That stone,' said the latter, 'I *must* have. I will pay you whatever you ask. But if you are not prepared to sell it to me, your Emperor, then you must leave my kingdom and the lands which I rule for ever and ever.'

Poor Lucius was left with no choice, so he handed the stone over to the royal hands and received five great sacks of gold in return.

Just as he was leaving the Emperor's presence, he heard the Imperial voice call out to him: 'Come back, my good fellow, and tell me how a poor woodcutter like yourself came into the possession of so rare a stone.'

'Well, Your Imperial Majesty, it was like this ...' and Lucius told the whole story from beginning to end.

The Emperor listened with ever-increasing anger and amazement and by the end he was almost trembling with fury. He rose to his feet and called out: 'Let the Lord Chamberlain be brought before me immediately.'

When Marcus arrived and saw Lucius standing in front of the Emperor, who was pale with rage, his knees began to knock together in fear and trembling.

'Is this good man's story true?' demanded the Emperor. 'Yes or no? Ah, I can see from your manner that the answer is yes and that you are indeed guilty of utterly shameful and disgraceful conduct, unworthy of a servant at my Court. You are not fit to live.'

But Lucius went down on his knees before the Emperor and pleaded for the cruel Lord Chamberlain's life. The Emperor was deeply moved by such generosity. 'You owe your life to this humble woodcutter,' he said to Marcus. 'My order now is that you be banished from my kingdom for ever.'

As for Lucius, he was given a post as Chief Guardian of the Imperial Forests and he lived happily with his wife to enjoy his wealth and position for many a long year.

The Baker's Daughter

O but the Baker's Daughter is beautiful!

The Baker's Daughter has yellow hair, and every night it is curled with rags, and every morning it stands out in a frizzy fluff round her head. The Baker's Daughter has blue dresses and pink dresses and spotted dresses, with flounces and flounces on them; she has beads around her neck and jingly bracelets and a ring with a real stone. All the girls in class sigh with envy of the Baker's Daughter.

But the Baker's Daughter is proud. She points her chin and she turns up her nose, and she is very, very superior. You never see her in the Baker's shop. She strolls up and down the sidewalk, sucking her beads.

You all know the Baker's shop, two steps down. It is warm in there, and busy. It smells of hot bread, and every few minutes the Baker, a hot untidy little man in shirt sleeves, comes up from the basement carrying a big tray of crullers, or shiny rolls, or twisted currant buns. The Baker works hard all day and he never has time to do more than just poke his nose outside the doorway, every hour or so, for a sniff of cool air. It is hard to believe that anything so beautiful as the Baker's Daughter could ever come out of the Baker's shop!

Once I started to write a poem. It began:

> O it is the Baker's Daughter,
> And she is grown so fair, so fair . . .

I thought I would make a very splendid valentine of it, all written out in a fine hand, with pink roses around and lots of

141

crinkly paper lace, and send it to her, secretly. But unfortunately I found out that it was too much like a poem that someone else wrote a long time ago, and so I have never finished it. But still it always comes into my mind whenever I see the Baker's Daughter sucking her beads.

There was only one thing in the Baker's shop that at all came up in magnificence to the Baker's Daughter herself, and that was the big round cake that sat right in the middle of the Baker's window. It was a chocolate cake, with all sorts of twirls and twiddles of lovely icing on it, and the word BIRTHDAY written in pink sugar letters. For some reason or other the Baker would never sell that cake. Perhaps he was afraid he would never be able to make another one quite so beautiful. He would sell you any other cake from his window but that one, and even if you went there very early on a Friday morning, which is cruller day, when there are no cakes at all, and asked him for a nice party cake, he would say:

'I can let you have one by three o'clock!'

And if you then asked, 'But how about the cake in the window?' he would reply:

'That's not for sale. You can have one by three o'clock!'

For though you should offer him dollars and dollars, he would never sell that cake!

I seldom dare to speak to the Baker's Daughter. I am much too humble. But she still has friends. Never little boys; these she points her chin at, from across the street. But there are little girls with whom she is on friendly terms for as much as a week at a time. Naturally they are very proud. If you can't be a princess or a movie star perhaps the next best thing is to be seen walking up to the drug-store soda fountain with the Baker's Daughter, and sitting there beside her on a tall stool eating pineapple sundae.

The Baker's Daughter

Now there was one little girl with whom the Baker's Daughter condescended at one time to be friends. Perhaps her name had something to do with it. She was called Carmelita Miggs, and Carmelita is a very romantic and superior name. She had black hair and a pair of bronze slippers, and she was the only little girl ever seen to stroll publicly with the Baker's Daughter, arm in arm. What they talked about no one knew. But Carmelita sometimes wore the Baker's Daughter's beads, and the Baker's Daughter would wear Carmelita's beads, and altogether they were very, very special friends while it lasted.

And it lasted until Carmelita had a birthday party.

The Baker's Daughter of course was invited, and several other of Carmelita's school friends. It was to be a real party, at four in the afternoon, with ice cream. And the Baker's Daughter said, very grandly, that she would bring a cake.

'I will bake you a nice one,' said her father, 'with orange icing on it. Now let me see . . . how many of you will there be?'

But that wasn't at all what the Baker's Daughter wanted. Anyone at all could bring a cake with orange icing. 'I will choose my own cake!' thought the Baker's Daughter.

But all she said was: 'That will be very nice!'

And in the afternoon while her father was down in the bake-shop kitchen putting the last twiddle on the orange cake (for he wanted to make it something very special), and while her mother was taking forty winks in the back room, and the bakery cat was sound asleep, with her four paws curled under her, behind the counter, the Baker's Daughter crept into the shop on tiptoe, in all her finery, and stole – yes, *stole* – that big magnificent cake from the very middle of the shop window!

You see, she had her eye on it, all along!

She lifted it up – and a nice, light cake it seemed – wooden

platter and all, and she covered it over with sheets of waxy paper and carried it round to Carmelita's house.

O but she looked proud, walking down the street with that big cake in her arms! Everyone turned to look at her.

'What a lovely cake!' cried all the little boys and girls when she arrived at Carmelita's house.

And the wrappings were taken off, very carefully, and it was set right in the middle of the table, with candles all around it.

'*What* a nice light cake!' said Carmelita's mother.

'All good cakes are light!' said the Baker's Daughter.

'It was very, very kind of your father to make such a splendid cake,' said Carmelita's mother.

'I chose it myself!' said the Baker's Daughter, tossing her head.

They talked a little, very politely, and Carmelita Miggs

showed all her birthday presents. And at last came the moment for the ice cream to be handed round on little glass plates.

'And now,' said Carmelita's mother, 'we'll all have some of that delicious cake!'

Carmelita had to cut it because it was her birthday. She stood there feeling very shy, for there was a great silence all round; everyone's eyes were fixed on the cake, and all one could hear was Tommy Bates busily sucking his ice-cream spoon, so as to get through first.

Only the Baker's Daughter sat there proudly, with her skirts spread out, looking indifferent, as though cakes like this were quite an everyday affair with her!

Carmelita took the knife and stuck it into the very middle of the pink icing, and pushed. You could have heard a pin drop.

But the knife didn't go in. Carmelita turned very red, and took a long breath and tried again. Still the knife wouldn't go in.

'You must try harder, dear,' said Carmelita's mother, smiling pleasantly. 'I expect the top icing is a little bit stiff! Do you want me to help you?'

Now Carmelita knew that she had been pushing just as hard as she could. It came upon her, all at once, that there must be something very, very queer about that cake! But she took another long breath, again, and this time her mother put *her* hand on the knife, too.

You could have heard *two* pins drop!

And then, suddenly, there was a funny 'plop', and the knife went in. And as it went in the cake slipped and turned a sort of somersault, and there it was, upside down, sticking on the tip of the knife that Carmelita's mother was still holding, and everyone looking most surprised. And that wasn't the worst of it!

It was all hollow inside!

In fact, it was just a big pasteboard shell covered over with icing, and *that* was why the Baker would never sell it to anyone!

Can you imagine how the party felt? How the little boys and girls whispered and giggled, how Carmelita wept and the Baker's Daughter grew redder and redder, and sniffier and sniffier, and how Carmelita's mother tried to smooth everything over and pretend that it was really all very funny, and quite the nicest thing that could happen at any birthday party? And how, at the very last minute, while the ice cream was melting away, they had to send out and buy a real cake, *somewhere else*!

But Carmelita Miggs didn't think it was a joke. She never, never forgave the Baker's Daughter for spoiling her party. For quite a long time she wouldn't speak to her at all. As for the other boys and girls, whenever they met Carmelita or the Baker's Daughter, they would say:

'Now we'll all have some cake!'

You would think, after this, that the Baker's Daughter would have changed her ways. But not a bit of it! I saw her, only the other day, strolling up and down the sidewalk and sucking her beads just as proud as ever.

As I went past I whispered very softly: 'Now we'll all have some cake!'

And do you know what the Baker's Daughter did? I hate to tell you.

She stuck – out – her – tongue!

There in the middle of the Baker's window, is another cake. This time it has green icing and pink roses, and two little sugar doves on top. It is even grander than the old one, and will probably last twice as long.

Unless, of course, someone else should have a birthday party!

A Necklace of Raindrops

A man called Mr Jones and his wife lived near the sea. One stormy night Mr Jones was in his garden when he saw the holly tree by his gate begin to toss and shake.

A voice cried, 'Help me! I'm stuck in the tree! Help me, or the storm will go on all night.'

Very surprised, Mr Jones walked down to the tree. In the middle of it was a tall man with a long grey cloak, and a long grey beard, and the brightest eyes you ever saw.

'Who are you?' Mr Jones said. 'What are you doing in my holly tree?'

'I got stuck in it, can't you see? Help me out, or the storm will go on all night. I am the North Wind, and it is my job to blow the storm away.'

So Mr Jones helped the North Wind out of the holly tree. The North Wind's hands were as cold as ice.

'Thank you,' said the North Wind. 'My cloak is torn, but never mind. You have helped me, so now I will do something for you.'

'I don't need anything,' Mr Jones said. 'My wife and I have a baby girl, just born, and we are as happy as any two people in the world.'

'In that case,' said the North Wind, 'I will be the baby's godfather. My birthday present to her will be this necklace of raindrops.'

From under his grey cloak he pulled out a fine, fine silver chain. On the chain were three bright, shining drops.

'You must put it round the baby's neck,' he said. 'The raindrops will not wet her, and they will not come off. Every year, on her birthday, I will bring her another drop. When she has four drops she will stay dry, even if she goes out in the hardest rainstorm. And when she has five drops no thunder or lightning can harm her. And when she has six drops she will not be blown away, even by the strongest wind. And when she has seven raindrops, she will be able to swim the deepest river. And when she has eight raindrops she will be able to swim the widest sea. And when she has nine raindrops she will be able to make the rain stop raining if she claps her hands. And when she has ten raindrops she will be able to make it start raining if she blows her nose.'

'Stop, stop!' cried Mr Jones. 'That is quite enough for one little girl!'

'I was going to stop anyway,' said the North Wind. 'Mind, she must never take the chain off, or it might bring bad luck. I must be off, now, to blow away the storm. I shall be back on her next birthday, with the fourth raindrop.'

And he flew away up into the sky, pushing the clouds before him so that the moon and stars could shine out.

Mr Jones went into his house and put the chain with the three raindrops round the neck of the baby, who was called Laura.

A year soon went by, and when the North Wind came back to the little house by the sea, Laura was able to crawl about, and to play with her three bright, shining raindrops. But she never took the chain off.

When the North Wind had given Laura her fourth rain-

drop she could not get wet, even if she was out in the hardest rain. Her mother would put her out in the garden in her pram, and people passing on the road would say, 'Look at that poor little baby, left out in all this rain. She will catch cold!'

But little Laura was quite dry, and quite happy, playing with the raindrops and waving to her godfather the North Wind as he flew over.

Next year he brought her her fifth raindrop. And the year after that, the sixth. And the year after that, the seventh. Now Laura could not be harmed by the worst storm, and if she fell into a pond or river she floated like a feather. And when she had eight raindrops she was able to swim across the widest sea – but as she was happy at home she had never tried.

And when she had nine raindrops Laura found that she could make the rain stop, by clapping her hands. So there were many, many sunny days by the sea. But Laura did not always clap her hands when it rained, for she loved to see the silver drops come sliding out of the sky.

Now it was time for Laura to go to school. You can guess how the other children loved her! They would call, 'Laura, Laura, make it stop raining, please, so that we can go out to play.'

And Laura always made the rain stop for them.

But there was a girl called Meg who said to herself, 'It isn't fair. Why should Laura have that lovely necklace and be able to stop the rain? Why shouldn't I have it?'

So Meg went to the teacher and said, 'Laura is wearing a necklace.'

Then the teacher said to Laura, 'You must take your necklace off in school, dear. That is the rule.'

'But it will bring bad luck if I take it off,' said Laura.

'Of course it will not bring bad luck. I will put it in a box for you and keep it safe till after school.'

So the teacher put the necklace in a box.

But Meg saw where she put it. And when the children were out playing, and the teacher was having her dinner, Meg went quickly and took the necklace and put it in her pocket.

When the teacher found that the necklace was gone, she was very angry and sad.

'Who has taken Laura's necklace?' she asked.

But nobody answered.

Meg kept her hand tight in her pocket, holding the necklace.

And poor Laura cried all the way home. Her tears rolled down her cheeks like rain as she walked along by the sea.

'Oh,' she cried, 'what will happen when I tell my godfather that I have lost his present?'

A fish put his head out of the water and said, 'Don't cry, Laura dear. You put me back in the sea when a wave threw me on the sand. I will help you find your necklace.'

And a bird flew down and called, 'Don't cry, Laura dear. You saved me when a storm blew me on to your roof and hurt my wing. I will help you find your necklace.'

And a mouse popped his head out of a hole and said, 'Don't cry, Laura dear. You saved me once when I fell in the river. I will help you find your necklace.'

So Laura dried her eyes. 'How will you help me?' she asked.

'I will look under the sea,' said the fish. 'And I will ask my brothers to help me.'

'I will fly about and look in the fields and woods and roads,' said the bird. 'And I will ask my brothers to help me.'

'I will look in the houses,' said the mouse. 'And I will ask my brothers to look in every corner and closet of every room in the world.'

So they set to work.

While Laura was talking to her three friends, what was Meg doing?

She put on the necklace and walked out in a rainstorm. But the rain made her very wet! And when she clapped her hands to stop it raining, the rain took no notice. It rained harder than ever.

The necklace would only work for its true owner.

So Meg was angry. But she still wore the necklace, until her father saw her with it on.

'Where did you get that necklace?' he asked.

'I found it in the road,' Meg said. Which was not true!

'It is too good for a child,' her father said. And he took it away from her. Meg and her father did not know that a little mouse could see them from a hole in the wall.

The mouse ran to tell his friends that the necklace was in Meg's house. And ten more mice came back with him to drag it away. But when they got there, the necklace was gone. Meg's father had sold it, for a great deal of money, to a silversmith. Two days later, a little mouse saw it in the silversmith's shop, and ran to tell his friends. But before the mice could come to take it, the silversmith had sold it to a trader who was buying fine and rare presents for the birthday of the Princess of Arabia.

Then a bird saw the necklace and flew to tell Laura.

'The necklace is on a ship, which is sailing across the sea to Arabia.'

'We will follow the ship,' said the fishes. 'We will tell you which way it goes. Follow us!'

But Laura stood on the edge of the sea.

'How can I swim all that way without my necklace?' she cried.

'I will take you on my back,' said a dolphin. 'You have often thrown me good things to eat when I was hungry.'

So the dolphin took her on his back, and the fishes went on in front, and the birds flew above, and after many days they came to Arabia.

'Now where is the necklace?' called the fishes to the birds.

'The King of Arabia has it. He is going to give it to the Princess for her birthday tomorrow.'

'Tomorrow is my birthday too,' said Laura. 'Oh, what will my godfather say when he comes to give me my tenth raindrop and finds that I have not got the necklace?'

The birds led Laura into the King's garden. And she slept all night under a palm tree. The grass was all dry, and the flowers were all brown, because it was so hot, and had not rained for a year.

Next morning the Princess came into the garden to open her presents. She had many lovely things: a flower that could sing, and a cage full of birds with green and silver feathers; a book that she could read for ever because it had no last page, and a cat who could play cat's cradle; a silver dress of spiderwebs and a gold dress of goldfish scales; a clock with a real cuckoo to tell the time, and a boat made out of a great pink shell. And among all the other presents was Laura's necklace.

When Laura saw the necklace she ran out from under the palm tree and cried, 'Oh, please, that necklace is mine!'

The King of Arabia was angry. 'Who is this girl?' he said. 'Who let her into my garden? Take her away and drop her in the sea!'

But the Princess, who was small and pretty, said, 'Wait a minute, Papa,' and to Laura she said, 'How do you know it is your necklace?'

'Because my godfather gave it to me! When I am wearing it I can go out in the rain without getting wet, no storm can harm me, I can swim any river and any sea, and I can make the rain stop raining.'

'But can you make it start to rain?' said the King.

'Not yet,' said Laura. 'Not till my godfather gives me the tenth raindrop.'

'If you can make it rain you shall have the necklace,' said the King. 'For we badly need rain in this country.'

But Laura was sad because she could not make it rain till she had her tenth raindrop.

Just then North Wind came flying into the King's garden.

'There you are, god-daughter!' he said. 'I have been looking all over the world for you, to give you your birthday present. Where is your necklace?'

'The Princess has it,' said poor Laura.

Then the North Wind was angry. 'You should not have taken it off!' he said. And he dropped the raindrop on to the dry grass, where it was lost. Then he flew away. Laura started to cry.

'Don't cry,' said the kind little Princess. 'You shall have the necklace back, for I can see it is yours.' And she put the chain over Laura's head. As soon as she did so, one of Laura's tears ran down and hung on the necklace beside the nine raindrops, making ten. Laura started to smile, she dried her eyes and blew her nose. And, guess what! as soon as she blew her nose, the rain began falling! It rained and it rained, the trees all spread out their leaves, and the flowers stretched their petals, they were so happy to have a drink.

155

At last Laura clapped her hands to stop the rain.

The King of Arabia was very pleased. 'That is the finest necklace I have ever seen,' he said. 'Will you come and stay with us every year, so that we have enough rain?' And Laura said she would do this.

Then they sent her home in the Princess's boat, made out of a pink shell. And the birds flew overhead, and the fishes swam in front.

'I am happy to have my necklace back,' said Laura. 'But I am even happier to have so many friends.'

What happened to Meg? The mice told the North Wind that she had taken Laura's necklace. And he came and blew the roof off her house and let in the rain, so she was SOAKING WET!

The Wild Swans

In a distant land, far, far away, where the swallows fly when we are having winter, there lived a king who had eleven sons and one daughter, Elisa. The eleven brothers went to school with stars on their breasts and swords at their sides. They did their writing on gold tablets, with pencils of diamond, and they knew their lessons just as well with their books as without. You could tell at once that they were princes. Their sister used to sit on a stool made of mirror-glass and had a picture-book which cost more than half a kingdom.

Oh, those children really did have a wonderful time, but alas it was not to be like that for long.

The king, their father, had married a second time and the new queen was a wicked queen who was not at all kind to the children – you could tell that from the very first day. There was great feasting and merrymaking on the wedding day and the children played at pretending to be visitors. But the new queen did not give them any of the delicious cakes or sweet apples that they usually got. No, she gave them sand in a teacup and told them to pretend with that.

The following week the queen sent little Elisa out into the country to stay with some peasants and before very long she had made the king believe so many false things about the poor princes that his heart was turned against them too, so that he even stopped caring about them.

'Fly out into the world and look after yourselves,' the evil queen told them. 'Fly out like great big birds which have no voices.' But still she could not do all the evil that she would have liked to do: the princes turned into eleven beautiful wild swans and with a curious cry they flew out through the palace windows over the park and into the woods.

It was still quite early in the morning when they came by the place where their sister Elisa lay sleeping in the peasants' hut. They soared above the roof, flapped their wings and turned their long necks this way and that, but no one heard or saw them, so they flew on and on, higher and higher into the clouds, far into the wide world and thence to a great dark forest that stretched right down the sea-shore.

Poor little Elisa was in the peasants' hut playing with a green leaf; that was the only toy she had. She made a hole in the leaf and looked at the sun through it and she felt she was looking at the bright eyes of her brothers; and whenever the warm sun shone on her cheeks, she thought of all their kisses.

And so the days went slowly by. The winds blowing through the rose-bushes outside the hut whispered to the roses: 'Who can be more beautiful than you?' And the roses shook their heads and replied, 'Elisa.' And when the old peasant woman sat by her doorway on Sunday reading from her hymn-book, the wind would rustle the pages saying, 'Who is gentler than you?' And the reply came, 'Elisa.' And what the roses and the hymn-book said was the pure truth.

When she reached the age of fifteen, Elisa was summoned back home to the palace. The queen saw how beautiful she was and she was filled with rage and hatred. She would certainly have liked to turn Elisa into a wild swan like her brothers but this she did not dare to do because the king wished to see his daughter.

Early in the morning the queen went to her bathroom, which was made of marble and adorned with soft cushions and splendid carpets. She fetched three toads, kissed them and said to one, 'Sit on Elisa's head when she gets into the bath so that she may become as slow-witted as you are.' And to the second toad she said, 'Sit upon her brow so that she may become so ugly that even her father will not recognize her.' And to the third toad she said, 'Rest upon her heart, so that her mind becomes evil and that she may suffer pain and torment.' And then she put the toads into the clear water (which immediately turned green), summoned Elisa, undressed her and made her get into the bath. As she sat in the bath, the first toad climbed into her hair, the second on to her forehead and the third on to her breast. Elisa did not seem to be aware of them, but when she stood up three red poppies were floating on the water. If the toads had not been poisonous and kissed by the witch, they would have changed into red roses. All the same, they were still flowers, and this was because they had been resting upon Elisa's head and heart. She was too gentle and innocent for witchcraft to have any real power over her.

When the evil queen saw this, she rubbed poor Elisa all over with walnut-juice so that she became a most unpleasant colour, and then she applied a vile ointment to Elisa's beautiful face and disarranged her hair so that it was a tangled mess. No one could possibly have recognized Elisa now. And so when her father saw her he really had quite a fright and said she wasn't his daughter at all. Nor would anyone have anything to do with her except the watchdog and the swallow, but these poor creatures had nothing to say to her.

The unhappy child wept and thought of her eleven brothers, who were all so far away. With great sadness in her heart she crept out of the palace and for the whole day she wandered over fields and moors and then into the great forest. She did not in the least know where she wanted to go but she felt so downcast and longed so much to see her brothers who, like herself, had been driven out into the wide world, that her only wish was to search until she found them.

She was now far from any road or path, and as it was getting dark she said her prayers and lay down on the soft moss, resting her head against the stump of a tree. The air was mild and still and all around, in the grass and moss, there were hundreds of glow-worms, gleaming like some green fire. And when she happened to touch a bough with her hand they fell like falling stars around where she lay. All that night she dreamed of her brothers. They were children again, playing together, writing on their golden slates with their diamond pencils and reading their wonderful picture-book, which had cost half a kingdom. But they weren't writing letters and words as they used to formerly; no, they were writing about their bold exploits and all the exciting things they had seen and done. And in the picture-book everything seemed to come alive: the birds sang and the people stepped out of the pages and spoke to Elisa and her brothers.

When she awoke the sun was high in the heavens. She couldn't see it properly through the dense branches of the tall trees; the sun's rays were dancing upon them like fluttering gold gauze. The air was scented with the smell of fresh green grass and the birds very nearly came and perched on her shoulders. She could hear the sounds of water splashing, and through an opening in the bushes Elisa could see it – so beautifully clear that every single leaf was reflected in it.

But when she saw her own face in the water she was very frightened, it was so dirty and ugly. Then she dipped her hand in the water and rubbed her eyes and forehead and lo! her skin gleamed white again! She took off her clothes and bathed in the cool, clear water, after which there was no more beautiful princess than Elisa in the whole wide world.

When she was dressed once more and her hair all smoothly plaited, she ran to the sparkling spring and drank from the palm of her hand. Then she wandered further into the forest, not quite knowing where she was going.

Everything was so perfectly still she could hear her own footsteps and every withered leaf as it crushed under her feet. There were no birds; at any rate, she couldn't see any. Nor could she feel any sunrays, for the foliage was so rich and dense. She lay down to sleep in the darkness of the forest, thinking all the time of her brothers and wondering if she would ever find them.

The next morning she got up and continued her walk through the forest. She met an old woman carrying a basket of berries. The woman gave her a few and then Elisa asked her whether she had seen eleven princes riding through the forest.

'No, my dear, I have not,' replied the old woman, 'but yesterday I did see eleven swans with golden crowns on their heads swimming down the river not far from this very spot.' And she led Elisa a little further on towards a slope. At the bottom of this slope was a winding brook. Elisa thanked the old woman and then continued to walk along the brook till it finally opened out on to the wide sea-shore. She stared for a long while at the innumerable pebbles on the beach, all washed round and smooth by the water. 'The sea never seems to get tired,' thought Elisa. 'Its waters keep rolling on, making the rough stones smooth, and I, too, will not tire in my search for my dear brothers.'

Scattered among the seaweed washed up by the tide she found eleven swans' feathers, which she gathered up into a little bundle. The tiny drops of water on them might have been dew or perhaps tears – she could not tell. Strangely enough, she did not feel lonely as she watched the ever-changing colours of the sea. A great black cloud floated by, and the sea seemed to say, 'I, too, can look angry.'

Just as the sun was setting Elisa saw seven wild swans with gold crowns on their heads flying towards the land. Like a long ribbon of white they came in, one behind the other, and Elisa climbed up the slope and hid behind a bush. The swans alighted quite close to her, flapping their great white wings.

As the sun disappeared into the water, the swans' skins peeled off and, lo and behold! there stood Elisa's brothers, eleven handsome princes. She gave a loud happy cry and sprang into their arms and called them by their names. And how happy the princes were to see their little sister once more, although she had now grown taller and more beautiful. They laughed and wept and soon they understood how wickedly their stepmother had treated them.

'We brothers,' said the eldest, 'fly about like wild swans as long as the sun is in the heavens. But when it sets, we assume our human shape. And so at sunset we must always take care to see that we are standing on our feet, for if we were flying then, in the clouds, we would come plunging down into the depths below. We do not live here. On the far side of the water there is a land as fine as this, but it is a long, long way away. We have to fly across the wide sea and there is no island where we could spend the night. There is but one solitary rock which juts out above the water, but it is not very big, and only standing side by side can we rest on it. If the sea is rough the water leaps up and sprays right over us. But still we are most thankful that this rock is there – and that is where we spend the night in our human shape. If it were not for this rock, we could never visit our homeland, because our journey takes two whole days. Only once a year are we permitted to visit our father's home for a short stay of eleven days. We fly over this great forest and we can see the palace where we were born and where our father lives. And we can also see the bell-tower of the church where our mother is buried. But now we have only two more days left and then we must depart, away over the sea to another beautiful land which is not our home. But how can we take you with us? We have neither ship nor boat . . .'

'And how shall I free you?' asked Elisa. And all night long they went on talking without finding an answer, and they slept only for a very short while.

Elisa was awakened by the sound of swans' wings flapping above her. Her brothers had once again been transformed and she saw them rising higher in ever widening circles and flying farther and farther away. But the youngest one stayed behind. He laid his swan's head on her lap and she caressed his white wings. Towards nightfall the other brothers came back and after sunset they were once again in their human form.

'When we leave you tomorrow, dear Elisa,' they said, 'we dare not return for a whole year. Have you the courage to come with us? All our wings together are strong enough to fly you over the sea with us.'

'Yes,' said Elisa, 'take me with you.'

They spent the whole night weaving a net out of supple willow bark and tough reeds and rushes. Elisa lay down on it and when the sun rose and the brothers changed into wild swans, they seized the net in their beaks and flew high up into the clouds with their dear sister, who was sound asleep. The sun's rays fell on her face, so one of the swans flew above her head to shade her with his broad wings.

When Elisa opened her eyes they were a long way from land, and she thought she was still dreaming, because it was such a strange feeling to be carried high up above the sea through the clouds. By her side lay a branch of lovely ripe berries and a handful of appetizing roots. These had been gathered by her youngest brother and placed there for her to eat. She sent him a grateful smile, for she recognized him as the one who flew above her to shade her with his wings.

They were now flying so high that the first ship they saw below them looked like a white seagull on the water. Behind them Elisa saw a huge cloud, like some gigantic mountain, and upon it were cast giant shadows of herself and of the eleven swans. It was a strange spectacle, the like of which she had never seen before, but as the sun rose higher in the heavens and the cloud was left behind the phantom shadows disappeared.

All that day they flew on and on but because they had their sister to carry they could not fly as swiftly as they usually did. But as the sun began to sink and the evening came near, Elisa was filled with a terrible fear, for she could not see their lonely rock anywhere in sight. To add to her terror, a fearful storm was gathering and she felt guilty because she thought her weight was slowing up the pace of the swans. Panic seized her as she thought of them turning into men and crashing down into the sea far below. She murmured a prayer to soothe her fears but she could still see no sign of the lonely rock. Flashes of lightning followed one another in quick succession and mighty gusts of wind drove menacing black clouds towards them.

Suddenly the swans made a downward plunge ... and Elisa thought this was the end, but soon they were flying straight on again, with the sun more than half below the water. It was only then that she first caught sight of the lonely rock – it was hardly bigger than a seal's head sticking out above the waves. The sun was sinking fast and was just about to disappear altogether below the water when she felt her foot touching the firm ground and she found herself in the midst of her brothers, all standing close together, arm in arm, on the rock. There was just enough space for the twelve of them. The storm still raged and the sea dashed with terrifying violence against their rock-refuge, but they stood firm and felt no fear.

By dawn the storm had died down and as soon as the sun rose the swans flew off from the rock, carrying Elisa with them. Ahead of them they saw a kind of mountain-land, covered almost entirely in ice, and in the centre a mighty palace, towering high and extending more than a mile in length. But this was not the land they were making for. The swans told Elisa that this was the ever-changing cloud palace of the Fairy Morgana, which no human being was ever allowed to enter. Even as Elisa gazed at it, the mountains and palace crumbled to pieces and in their place rose golden-spired churches. And then again, even as she admired the churches, they changed into a fleet of ships. Then the scene altered once more, and then once again, until finally and suddenly there loomed up a range of magnificent blue mountains, cedar forests and turreted castles. And before the sun had set, Elisa found herself seated on a rock in front of a great cavern covered with delicate creeper. Her youngest brother led her into the cavern. 'Here you shall sleep,' he said to her. 'Perhaps tonight you may dream of a way of freeing us.'

'Heaven grant that I may!' said Elisa. And as she lay down to sleep she sent up a prayer. And the dream she dreamt that night was of the Fairy Morgana and the cloud palace over which she had flown with her brothers. The Fairy came out to meet her, enchantingly beautiful, but somehow looking like the old woman who had offered her berries in the forest and who had told her of the swans with the golden crowns.

'You have the power to set your brothers free,' she said, 'but have you the courage to persevere? Do you see these stinging nettles I hold in my hand? They have been picked from among those that grow out of churchyard graves, and these only are the kind that will be of use to you. Mark that well! They will burn blisters on your skin, but you must not mind that, however painful it may be. Then you must tread on them with your bare feet to break them up and make them into flax. This you will bind and twist and weave into eleven shirts with long sleeves for your brothers. When you throw these shirts over the wild swans, the spell will break. But mark this well! From the moment you start your task and until it is complete, *you must not speak*. The very first word you utter will pierce your brothers' hearts like a deadly dagger. Their lives hang on your tongue. Mark that well!'

And then she touched Elisa's hand with the nettle. It was as though a flame burned into her and she awoke with the pain.

It was daylight and close by where she had been sleeping was a nettle like the one she had seen in her dreams. She left the cave to begin her heavy task. On the churchyard graves she sought out the nettles with her delicate hands. They burnt like fire and raised great blisters on her hands and arms, but she did not mind the pain because she knew she was thus helping to free her beloved brothers. With her bare feet she trod down every nettle and then twisted and bound the green flax.

When the sun set her brothers returned and when they found Elisa so silent they were frightened and didn't know what to think. Was it some new spell cast upon her by their evil step-mother? But when they saw her blistered hands, they realized she must be doing it for their sake. The youngest brother wept bitter tears and where his tears fell, she felt no more pain and the blisters disappeared.

All through the night she went on with her task, for she could have no rest till she had freed her brothers. And all next day, when the swans were away, she sat in silent solitude. She had now finished one shirt and was at work on the second.

While she was thus occupied she heard the sound of a hunting-horn echoing through the mountains, together with with the baying of hounds. Fearful, Elisa took refuge in a cave, gathering her nettles into a bundle and hiding them. A great hound leapt out from among the bushes, followed by another and then another. They bayed and kept running backwards and forwards. Soon a whole band of hunters were outside the cave and one of them, he seemed to be the tallest and most handsome, came towards Elisa. Never had he beheld a more beautiful girl.

'How come you to be in this cave, fair maiden?' asked the king (for indeed he was the king). But Elisa simply shook her head and said not a word, for she knew that if she spoke it would cost her brothers their lives.

'Follow me,' said the king, 'you may not stay here. If you are as good as you are beautiful, I will clothe you in silks and velvets and set a golden crown on your head and you shall come and live in my grandest palace.' And the king lifted her up on to his horse. Elisa wept and wrung her hands, but as they rode off through the mountains, followed by the huntsmen, he said to her, 'It is only your happiness I want. One day you will thank me.'

The sun was now setting and in front of them lay the splendid royal city with its churches and domes. The king led Elisa to the palace but she had no eyes for its magnificence and sumptuous beauty. She wept and felt nothing would relieve her grief. The women of the palace dressed her in rich regal robes, threaded precious pearls into her long hair and sheathed her hands and arms in long, delicately woven gloves but Elisa remained indifferent to their attentions.

Even so, when she was finally arrayed in all her splendid attire, the whole court was speechless before her dazzling beauty and the king chose her to be his bride. But the archbishop shook his head, muttering in the king's ear that the beautiful forest-girl was a sorceress who had bewitched the whole court and cast a spell on the king's heart.

But the king refused to listen to him and commanded that a sumptuous banquet be prepared and joyous music played, though he was sadly disappointed to see that Elisa remained as downcast and sorrowful as ever.

Then the king led her to a small room adorned with the loveliest green hangings; it looked very much like the cave where the king had first seen her. From the ceiling hung the one shirt which she had finished weaving and on the floor was the bundle of flax she had spun from the nettles.

'Dear child,' said the king, 'in this room you can occupy yourself with the work you were doing before. You can imagine you are back in your old home.'

When Elisa saw these familiar things, a smile came to her lips and the colour to her cheeks. She kissed the king's hand

and he pressed her to him. He then left and gave the order for the church bells to peal in honour of the forthcoming royal wedding. The beautiful dumb forest-girl was soon to be crowned queen.

However, the archbishop continued to mutter evil things about Elisa into the king's ear and to spread rumours in the court. The king took little notice and the marriage was soon celebrated with all pomp and ceremony. The archbishop himself, according to the custom of the land, had to place the crown on Elisa's head and he pressed it down so hard that it hurt. But there was so much sadness in her heart for her brothers that she felt no pain and no sound came from her lips.

The king was exceedingly kind to her and did all he could to help her; and she came to love him more and more every day. She would most dearly have liked to tell him of her sufferings, but she dared not utter a word until her task was completed. Each night she would slip from his side and return to the little green room and continue to weave the shirts for her beloved brothers. But when she started on the seventh shirt, she found she had no more flax left. She knew she must go down to the churchyard to pick the stinging nettles with her own hand, but how was she to get there? By the light of the moon she tiptoed out into the garden, through the long dark paths and out into the churchyard that lay behind the garden. On one of the tombstones sat a circle of hideous-looking witches. They took off their ragged clothing as though they were about to bathe, and with their long skinny fingers they prised open the newly dug graves, drew out the dead bodies and devoured the flesh. They fixed their evil eyes on Elisa as she passed but she said a silent prayer and they could not harm her. She collected the burning nettles and crept back to the palace.

But one person had seen her, and that was the archbishop, who had remained awake while everybody else lay asleep. He was now certain that the new queen was a witch, using some evil sorcery to make the king and all his people do as she wanted.

The archbishop went and told the king what he had seen and how sure he was that the dumb, beautiful forest girl was in reality a sorceress. The king did not know what to say. He looked round the church and saw the carved wooden images of the saints on the walls. They seemed to be gravely shaking their heads and saying, 'No, Elisa is innocent.' But the archbishop insisted that what they were really saying was that Elisa was guilty. Tears rolled down the king's cheeks and his heart became heavy with doubt. That night he could not sleep, but he pretended to be sleeping and he saw Elisa get up in the middle of the night and go into the small green room.

The same thing happened the next night, and the next. Day by day the king's heart grew sadder and Elisa saw this but did not understand why.

By this time she had almost finished ten shirts and then only one more would remain to be done. But she had no more flax left and, worse still, she had no more stinging nettles. So once more she was forced to go down to the churchyard. The archbishop and the king followed her and saw her pass the hideous witches sitting on one of the tombstones. The king had to turn his face away, for he imagined Elisa to be one of them.

'The people of the land must judge her,' said the king the next day. And the people judged Elisa and decided that she must be burned in fire like a witch.

Elisa was taken from the palace and led to a dark, damp dungeon, where the wind whistled through the barred windows. They allowed her the nettles she had gathered to use as a pillow, and the shirts she had woven as quilts and blankets. Nothing more dear and more precious than these could have been given to her.

Outside the prison street boys sang jeering songs and there was no one to comfort her with a kind word.

But that evening the youngest of the swans suddenly came flapping his wings outside her barred window, and Elisa wept, for she knew that this night might be the last she had left to live. But now her task was nearly complete and her brothers were there. The archbishop came and tried to speak to her, but she waved him away with looks and gestures, for nothing must be allowed to interrupt her work. Her tears and pain must not have been in vain, and so the archbishop departed, muttering evil words. But Elisa knew she was innocent and continued her work.

It was still one hour before daybreak next morning when her eleven brothers came to the palace gate and demanded to be taken to the presence of the king. They were told that his Majesty was still asleep and must not be disturbed. The brothers begged and pleaded and even threatened the palace guards. At long last the king came out.

'What is the meaning of all this?' he asked. Just at that moment the sun rose and the brothers vanished but eleven swans could be seen flying away.

And now all the people came streaming out of their houses to witness the burning of the witch. Elisa was put in an old cart and dressed in a shift of coarse cloth. She was deathly pale and her lovely long hair hung unkempt about her face. Her lips moved in silent prayer while her hands did not cease weaving away at the eleventh shirt. Even on her way to her death she did not interrupt her work.

The people screamed and shouted at her. 'See how the witch mutters! Look at her sitting there with her vile sorcery! Tear it from her! Tear it into a thousand pieces!'

Just as the mob was getting more and more fierce and surging furiously towards the cart, the eleven swans came flapping down towards her. They perched themselves around her on the cart and fluttered their great wings. The mob were frightened and gave way before them, whispering among themselves, 'This is a sign from heaven. She must be innocent.' But they dared not say this aloud. And now the hangman seized Elisa by the hand, but she quickly threw the eleven shirts one after the other over the swans and lo! in their place stood eleven tall, handsome princes! The youngest had a swan's wing instead of an arm, because a sleeve was missing to his shirt, which she had not quite finished.

'Now I can speak!' cried Elisa. 'I am innocent!'

The crowd of people went down on their knees as though before a saint, and then Elisa sank, almost lifeless, into her brother's arms.

'Yes, she is indeed innocent,' cried the eldest brother. And then he told them everything that had happened to them and to her.

Then a wonderful thing took place. Out of the pile of wood and sticks, where Elisa was to have been burned, there rose the sweet scent of myriads of roses. Every single stick had taken root and put out branches; the funeral pyre was now a tall hedge of glistening red roses. There was one that grew out taller and more stately than the rest and this one the king plucked and laid it on Elisa's breast. She opened her eyes, which were now filled with peace and happiness.

Then the church bells pealed out as never before and the king, followed by the eleven princes and great crowds of people, led his queen back to the royal palace.

The Tale of the Silver Saucer and the Transparent Apple

There was once an old peasant; he was a merchant, and used to take things every year to sell at the big fair of Nijni Novgorod; and he had three daughters. They were none of them so bad to look at, but one of them was very pretty. And she was the best of them too. The others put all the hard work on her, while they did nothing but look at themselves in the looking-glass and complain of what they had to eat. They called the pretty one 'Little Stupid', because she was so good and did all their work for them. Oh, they were real bad ones, those two.

Well, the time came round for the merchant to pack up and go to the big fair. He called his daughters, and said, 'Little pigeons, what would you like me to bring you from the fair?'

Says the eldest, 'I'd like a necklace, but it must be a rich one.'

Says the second, 'I want a new dress with gold hems.'

But the youngest, the good one, Little Stupid, said nothing at all.

'Now, little one,' says her father, 'what is it you want? I must bring something for you too.'

Says the little one, 'Could I have a silver saucer and a transparent apple? But never mind if there are none.'

The old merchant says, 'Long hair, short sense,' but he promised the little pretty one, who was so good that her sisters called her stupid, that if he could get her a silver saucer and a transparent apple she should have them.

Then they all kissed each other, and he cracked his whip, and off he went, with the little bells jingling on the horses' harness.

The three sisters waited till he came back. The two elder ones looked in the looking-glass, and thought how fine they would look in the new necklace and the new dress; but the little pretty one took care of her old mother, and scrubbed and dusted and swept and cooked, and every day the other two said that the soup was burnt or the bread was not properly baked.

Then one day there was a jingling of bells and a clattering of horses' hoofs, and the old merchant came driving back from the fair.

The sisters ran out.

'Where is the necklace?' asked the first.

'You haven't forgotten the dress?' asked the second.

But the little one, Little Stupid, helped her old father off with his coat, and asked him if he was tired.

'Well, little one,' says the old merchant, 'and don't you want your fairing too? I went from one end of the market to the other before I could get what you wanted. I bought the silver saucer from an old Jew, and the transparent apple from a Finnish hag.'

'O, thank you, father,' says the little one.

'And what will you do with them?' says he.

'I shall spin the apple in the saucer,' says the little pretty one, and at that the old merchant burst out laughing.

'They don't call you "Little Stupid" for nothing,' says he.

Well, they all had their fairings, and the two elder sisters, the bad ones, they ran off and put on the new dress and the new necklace, and came out and strutted about, preening themselves like herons, now on one leg and now on the other, to see how they looked. But Little Stupid, she just sat herself down beside the stove, and took the transparent apple and set it in the silver saucer, and she laughed softly to herself. And then she began spinning the apple in the saucer.

Round and round the apple spun in the saucer, faster and faster, till you couldn't see the apple at all, nothing but a mist like a little whirlpool in the silver saucer. And the little good one looked at it, and her eyes shone.

Her sisters laughed at her.

'Spinning an apple in a saucer and staring at it, the little stupid,' they said, as they strutted about the room, listening to the rustle of the new dress and fingering the bright round stone of the necklace.

But the little pretty one did not mind them. She sat in the corner watching the spinning apple. And as it spun she talked to it.

'Spin, spin, apple in the silver saucer.' That is what she said. 'Spin so that I may see the world. Let me have a peep at the little father Tzar on his high throne. Let me see the rivers and the ships and the great towns far away.'

And as she looked at the little glass whirlpool in the saucer, there was the Tzar, the Little Father – God preserve him! – sitting on his high throne. Ships sailed on the seas, their white sails swelling in the wind. There was Moscow with its white stone walls and painted churches. Why, there were the market at Nijni Novgorod, and the Arab merchants with their camels, and the Chinese with their blue trousers and bamboo staves. And then there was the great river Volga, with men on the banks towing ships against the stream. Yes, and she saw a sturgeon asleep in a deep pool.

'Oh! oh! oh!' says the little pretty one as she saw all these things.

And the bad ones, they saw how her eyes shone, and they came and looked over her shoulder, and saw how all the world was there, in the spinning apple and the silver saucer. And the old father came and looked over her shoulder too, and he saw the market at Nijni Novgorod.

'Why, there is the inn where I put up the horses,' says he. 'You haven't done so badly after all, Little Stupid.'

And the little pretty one, Little Stupid, went on staring into the glass whirlpool in the saucer, spinning the apple, and seeing all the world she had never seen before, floating there before her in the saucer, brighter than leaves in the sunlight.

The bad ones, the elder sisters, were sick with envy.

'Little Stupid,' says the first, 'if you will give me your silver saucer and your transparent apple, I will give you my fine new necklace.'

'Little Stupid,' says the second, 'I will give you my new dress with gold hems if you will give me your transparent apple and your silver saucer.'

'Oh, I couldn't do that,' says the Little Stupid, and she goes on spinning the apple in the saucer and seeing what was happening all over the world.

So the bad ones put their wicked heads together and thought of a plan. And they took their father's axe, and went into the deep forest and hid it under a bush.

The next day they waited till afternoon, when work was

done, and the little pretty one was spinning her apple in the saucer. Then they said –

'Come along, Little Stupid; we are all going to gather berries in the forest.'

'Do you really want me to come too?' says the little one. She would rather have played with her apple and saucer.

But they said, 'Why, of course. You don't think we can carry all the berries ourselves!'

So the little one jumped up, and found the baskets, and went with them to the forest. But before she started she ran to her father, who was counting his money and was not too pleased to be interrupted, for figures go quickly out of your head when you have a lot to remember. She asked him to take care of the silver saucer and the transparent apple for fear she would lose them in the forest.

'Very well, little bird,' says the old man, and he put the things in a box with a lock and key to it. He was a merchant, and that sort are always careful about things, and go clattering about with a lot of keys at their belt.

So the little one picks up all three baskets and runs off after the others, the bad ones, with black hearts under their necklaces and new dresses.

They went deep into the forest, picking berries, and the little one picked so fast that she soon had a basket full. She was picking and picking, and did not see what the bad ones were doing. They were fetching the axe.

The little one stood up to straighten her back, which ached after so much stooping, and she saw her two sisters standing in front of her, looking at her cruelly. Their baskets lay on the ground quite empty. They had not picked a berry. The eldest had the axe in her hand.

The little one was frightened.

The Tale of the Silver Saucer and the Transparent Apple

'What is it, sisters?' says she; 'and why do you look at me with cruel eyes? And what is the axe for? You are not going to cut berries with an axe.'

'No, Little Stupid,' says the first, 'we are not going to cut berries with the axe.'

'No, Little Stupid,' says the second; 'the axe is here for something else.'

The little one begged them not to frighten her.

Says the first, 'Give me your transparent apple.'

Says the second, 'Give me your silver saucer.'

'If you don't give them up at once, we shall kill you.' That is what the bad ones said.

The poor little one begged them, 'O darling sisters, do not kill me! I haven't got the saucer or the apple with me at all.'

'What a lie!' say the bad ones. 'You never would leave it behind.'

And one caught her by the hair, and the other swung the axe, and between them they killed the little pretty one, who was called Little Stupid because she was so good.

Then they looked for the saucer and the apple, and could not find them. But it was too late now. So they made a hole in the ground, and buried the little one under a birch tree.

When the sun went down the bad ones came home, and they wailed with false voices, and rubbed their eyes to make the tears come. They made their eyes red and their noses too, and they did not look any prettier for that.

'What is the matter with you, little pigeons?' said the old merchant and his wife. I would not say 'little pigeons' to such bad ones. Black-hearted crows is what I would call them.

And they wail and lament aloud –

'We are miserable for ever. Our poor little sister is lost. We looked for her everywhere. We heard the wolves howling. They must have eaten her.'

The old mother and father cried like rivers in springtime, because they loved the little pretty one, who was called Little Stupid because she was so good.

But before their tears were dry the bad ones began to ask for the silver saucer and the transparent apple.

'No, no,' says the old man; 'I shall keep them for ever in memory of my poor little daughter whom God has taken away.'

So the bad ones did not gain by killing their little sister.

Time did not stop with the death of the little girl. Winter came, and the snow with it. Everything was all white, just as it is now. And the wolves came to the doors of the huts, even into the villages, and no one stirred farther than he need. And then the snow melted, and buds broke on the trees, and the birds began singing, and the sun shone warmer every day. The old people had almost forgotten the little pretty one who lay dead in the forest. The bad ones had not forgotten, because now they had to do the work, and they did not like that at all.

And then one day some lambs strayed away into the forest, and a young shepherd went after them to bring them safely back to their mothers. And as he wandered this way and that through the forest, following their light tracks, he came to a little birch tree, bright with new leaves, waving over a little mound of earth. And there was a reed growing in the mound, and that is a strange thing, one reed all by itself under a birch tree in the forest. But it was no stranger than the flowers round it, some red as the sun at dawn and others blue as the summer sky.

Well, the shepherd looks at the reed, and he looks at those

flowers, and he thinks, 'I've never seen anything like that before. I'll make a whistle-pipe of that reed, and keep it for a memory till I grow old.'

So he did. He cut the reed, and sat himself down on the mound, and carved away at the reed with his knife, and got the pith out of it by pushing a twig through it, and, beating it gently till the bark swelled, made holes in it, and there was his whistle-pipe. And then he put it to his lips to see what sort of music he could make on it. But that he never knew, for before his lips touched it the whistle-pipe began playing by itself and reciting in a girl's sweet voice. This is what it sang:

'Play, play, whistle-pipe. Bring happiness to my dear father and to my little mother. I was killed – yes, my life was taken from me in the deep forest for the sake of a silver saucer, for the sake of a transparent apple.'

When he heard that the shepherd went back quickly to the village to show it to the people. And all the way the whistle-pipe went on playing and reciting, singing its little song. And everyone who heard it said, 'What a strange song! But who is it who was killed?'

'I know nothing about it,' says the shepherd, and he tells them about the mound and the reed and the flowers, and how he cut the reed and made the whistle-pipe, and how the whistle-pipe does its playing by itself.

And as he was going through the village, with all the people crowding about him, the old merchant, that one who was the father of the two bad ones and of the little pretty one, came along and listened with the rest. And when he heard the words about the silver saucer and the transparent apple, he snatched the whistle-pipe from the shepherd boy. And still it sang:

'Play, play, whistle-pipe! Bring happiness to my dear father and to my little mother. I was killed – yes, for my life was taken from me in the deep forest for the sake of a silver saucer, for the sake of a transparent apple.'

And the old merchant remembered the little good one, and his tears trickled over his cheeks and down his old beard. And he said to the shepherd –

'Take me at once to the mound, where you say you cut the reed.'

The shepherd led the way, and the old man walked beside him, crying, while the whistle-pipe in his hand went on singing and reciting its little song over and over again.

They came to the mound under the birch tree, and there were the flowers, shining red and blue, and there in the middle of the mound was the stump of the reed which the shepherd had cut.

The whistle-pipe sang on and on.

Well, there and then they dug up the mound, and there was the little girl lying under the dark earth as if she were asleep.

'O God of mine,' says the old merchant, 'this is my daughter, my little pretty one, whom we called Little Stupid.' He began to weep loudly and wring his hands; but the whistle-pipe, playing and reciting, changed its song. This is what it sang:

'My sisters took me into the forest to look for the red berries. In the deep forest they killed poor me for the sake of a silver saucer, for the sake of a transparent apple. Wake me, dear father, from a bitter dream, by fetching water from the well of the Tzar.'

How the people scowled at the two sisters! They scowled, they cursed them for the bad ones they were. And the bad ones, the two sisters, wept, and fell on their knees, and con-

fessed everything. They were taken, and their hands were tied, and they were shut up in prison.

'Do not kill them,' begged the old merchant, 'for then I should have no daughters at all, and when there are no fish in the river we make shift with crays. Besides, let me go to the Tzar and beg water from his well. Perhaps my daughter will wake up, as the whistle-pipe tells us.'

And the whistle-pipe sang again:

'Wake me, wake me, dear father, from a bitter dream, by fetching water from the well of the Tzar. Till then, dear father, a blanket of black earth and the shade of the green birch tree.'

So they covered the little girl with her blanket of earth, and the shepherd with his dogs watched the mound night and day. He begged for the whistle-pipe to keep him company, poor lad, and all the days and nights he thought of the sweet face of the little pretty one he had seen there under the birch tree.

The old merchant harnessed his horse, as if he were going to the town; and he drove off through the forest, along the roads, till he came to the palace of the Tzar, the Little Father of all good Russians. And then he left his horse and cart and waited on the steps of the palace.

The Tzar, the Little Father, with rings on his fingers and a gold crown on his head, came out on the steps in the morning sunshine; and as for the old merchant, he fell on his knees and kissed the feet of the Tzar, and begged –

'O Little Father, Tzar, give me leave to take water – just a little drop of water – from your holy well.'

'And what will you do with it?' says the Tzar.

'I will wake my daughter from a bitter dream,' says the old merchant. 'She was murdered by her sisters – killed in the deep forest – for the sake of a silver saucer, for the sake of a transparent apple.'

'A silver saucer?' says the Tzar – 'a transparent apple? Tell me about that.'

And the old merchant told the Tzar everything, just as I have told it to you.

And the Tzar, the Little Father, he gave the old merchant a glass of water from his holy well. 'But,' says he, 'when your daughterkin wakes, bring her to me, and her sisters with her, and also the silver saucer and the transparent apple.'

The old man kissed the ground before the Tzar, and took the glass of water and drove home with it, and I can tell you he was careful not to spill a drop. He carried it all the way in one hand as he drove.

He came to the forest and to the flowering mound under the little birch tree, and there was the shepherd watching with his dogs. The old merchant and the shepherd took away the blanket of black earth. Tenderly, tenderly, the shepherd used his fingers, until the little girl, the pretty one, the good one, lay there as sweet as if she were not dead.

Then the merchant scattered the holy water from the glass over the little girl. And his daughterkin blushed as she lay there, and opened her eyes, and passed a hand across them, as if she were waking from a dream. And then she leapt up, crying and laughing, and clung about her old father's neck. And there they stood, the two of them, laughing and crying with joy. And the shepherd could not take his eyes from her, and in his eyes too, there were tears.

But the old father did not forget what he had promised the Tzar. He set the little pretty one, who had been so good that her wicked sisters had called her Stupid, to sit beside him on the cart. And he brought something from the house in a coffer of wood, and kept it under his coat. And they brought out the two sisters, the bad ones, from their dark prison, and set them in the cart. And the Little Stupid kissed them and cried over them, and wanted to loose their hands, but the old merchant would not let her. And they all drove together till they came to the palace of the Tzar. The shepherd boy could not take his eyes from the little pretty one, and he ran all the way behind the cart.

Well, they came to the palace, and waited on the steps; and the Tzar came out to take the morning air, and he saw the old merchant, and the two sisters with their hands tied, and the little pretty one, as lovely as a spring day. And the Tzar saw her, and could not take his eyes from her. He did not see the shepherd boy, who hid away among the crowd.

Says the great Tzar to his soldiers, pointing to the bad sisters, 'These two are to be put to death at sunset. When the sun goes down their heads must come off, for they are not fit to see another day.'

Then he turns to the pretty one, and he says: 'Little sweet pigeon, where is your silver saucer, and where is your transparent apple?'

The old merchant took the wooden box from under his coat, and opened it with a key at his belt, and gave it to the little one, and she took out the silver saucer and the transparent apple and gave them to the Tzar.

'O lord Tzar,' says she, 'O Little Father, spin the apple in the saucer, and you will see whatever you wish to see – your soldiers, your high hills, your forests, your plains, your rivers, and everything in all Russia.'

And the Tzar, the Little Father, spun the apple in the saucer till it seemed a little whirlpool of white mist, and there he saw glittering towns, and regiments of soldiers marching to war, and ships, and day and night, and the clear stars above the trees. He looked at these things and thought much of them.

Then the little good one threw herself on her knees before him, weeping.

'O Little Father, Tzar,' she says, 'take my transparent apple and my silver saucer; only forgive my sisters. Do not kill them because of me. If their heads are cut off when the sun goes down, it would have been better for me to lie under the blanket of black earth in the shade of the birch tree in the forest.'

The Tzar was pleased with the kind heart of the little pretty one, and he forgave the bad ones, and their hands were untied, and the little pretty one kissed them, and they kissed her again and said they were sorry.

The old merchant looked up at the sun, and saw how the time was going.

'Well, well,' says he, 'it's time we were getting ready to go home.'

They all fell on their knees before the Tzar and thanked him. But the Tzar could not take his eyes from the little pretty one, and would not let her go.

'Little sweet pigeon,' says he, 'will you be my Tzaritza, and a kind mother to Holy Russia?'

And the little one did not know what to say. She blushed and answered, very rightly, 'As my father orders and as my little mother wishes, so shall it be.'

The Tzar was pleased with her answer, and he sent a messenger on a galloping horse to ask leave from the little pretty one's old mother. And of course the old mother said that she was more than willing. So that was all right. Then there was a wedding – such a wedding! – and every city in Russia sent a silver plate of bread, and a golden salt-cellar, with their good wishes to the Tzar and Tzaritza.

Only the shepherd boy, when he heard that the little pretty one was to marry the Tzar, turned sadly away and went off into the forest.

'Are you happy, little sweet pigeon?' says the Tzar.

'Oh, yes,' says the Little Stupid, who was now Tzaritza and mother of Holy Russia; 'but there is one thing that would make me happier.'

'And what is that?' says the lord Tzar.

'I cannot bear to lose my old father and my little mother and my dear sisters. Let them be with me here in the palace, as they were in my father's house.'

The Tzar laughed at the little pretty one, but he agreed, and the little pretty one ran to tell them the good news. She said to her sisters, 'Let all be forgotten, and all be forgiven, and may the evil eye fall on the one who first speaks of what has been!'

For a long time the Tzar lived, and the little pretty one the Tzaritza, and they had many children, and were very happy together.

Acknowledgements

We are most grateful to the undermentioned publishers and authors for permission to include the following stories:

The Butterfly that Stamped by Rudyard Kipling (from *Just So Stories*) is reprinted by permission of The National Trust.

Damian and the Dragon by Ruth Manning-Sanders is published by Methuen and Company Ltd.

The Cave of the Cyclops is by Philippa Pearce.

Boffy and the Teacher Eater by M. Stuart-Barry is published by George G. Harrap and Company Ltd.

Titus in Trouble by James Reeves is published by The Bodley Head.

The Rabbit Makes a Match by Kay Hill is published by McClelland and Stewart Ltd.

The Baker's Daughter by Margery Williams Bianco is published by Doubleday and Company.

A Necklace of Raindrops by Joan Aiken is published by Jonathan Cape Ltd.

The Tale of the Silver Saucer and the Transparent Apple from *Old Peter's Russian Tales* by Arthur Ransome is published by Hamish Hamilton Ltd.

We should like to thank the Children's Librarians of the London Borough of Barnet, Mary Junor, Schools Librarian, Barnet, and the staff of the Golders Green Library; Mrs S. Stonebridge, former Co-ordinator of Children's and Youth Services, Royal Borough of

Acknowledgements

Kensington and Chelsea, and Miss V. Newton, former Children's Librarian, Chelsea, for their ever-ready help. We are also very much indebted to our colleague Hazel Wilkinson and to Christine Carter, former Children's Librarian, Hertfordshire College of Higher Education.

Once more we record our gratitude to Phyllis Hunt of Faber and Faber for her painstaking care over detail and constant guidance and advice.